SIREN
Publishing

MARLA M

Ménage Everlasting

The
Teacher's
Pets

RIVERBEND, TEXAS HEAT 8

The Teacher's Pets

Wesson and Cole are attracted to Jessie. Can they convince her to give two men a try? Will she risk losing her job for them?

With someone shooting darts at the cattle, the men's attentions are divided between dating her and protecting their ranch. Neither man wants Jessie hurt, so when she is hit by a tranquilizer dart they feel responsible and panic.

Jessie has fallen for the two men and despite threats to her job teaching children, she continues to see them. They aren't taking any chances with her safety but never think that the threat could be closer to her than to them.

Finding out that the attacker is someone Jessie sees most every day only reinforces

the need to protect their woman. Wesson and Cole close ranks around her. Jessie loves that they are so protective of her. Once the threat is eliminated, she agrees to be their wife.

Genres: Contemporary, Ménage a Trois/Quatre, Romantic Suspense, Western/Cowboys

Length: 49,000

THE TEACHER'S PETS

Riverbend, Texas Heat 8

Marla Monroe

Siren Publishing, Inc.
www.SirenPublishing.com

A SIREN PUBLISHING BOOK

The Teacher's Pets
Copyright © 2018 by Marla Monroe
ISBN978-1-64243-543-6
First Publication: October 2018
Cover design by Les Byerley
All art and logo copyright © 2018 by Siren Publishing, Inc.

Siren Publishing, Inc.
www.SirenPublishing.com

ABOUT THE AUTHOR

Marla Monroe has been writing professionally for over thirteen years. Her first book with Siren was published in January of 2011, and she now has over 85 books available with them. She loves to write and spends every spare minute either at the keyboard or reading. She writes everything from sizzling-hot cowboys, emotionally charged BDSM, and dangerously addictive shifters, to science fiction ménages with the occasional badass biker thrown in for good measure.

Marla lives in the southern US and works full-time at a busy hospital. When not writing, she loves to travel, spend time with her feline muses, and read. Although she misses her cross-stitch and putting together puzzles, she is much happier writing fantasy worlds where she can make everyone's dreams come true. She's always eager to try something new and thoroughly enjoys the research she does for her books. She loves to hear from readers about what they are looking for in their reading adventures.

You can reach Marla at themarlamonroe@yahoo.com, or
Visit her website at www.marlamonroe.com
Her blog: www.themarlamonroe.blogspot.com
Twitter: @MarlaMonroe1
Facebook: www.facebook.com/marla.monroe.7
Google+: https://plus.google.com/u/0/+marlamonroe7/posts
Goodreads:
https://www.goodreads.com/author/show/4562866.Marla_Monroe
Pinterest: http://www.pinterest.com/marlamonroe/
BookStrand: http://bit.ly/MzcA6I
Amazon page: http://amzn.to/1euRooO

For all titles by Marla Monroe, please visit
www.bookstrand.com/marla-monroe

The Teacher's Pets

Riverbend, Texas Heat 8

MARLA MONROE
Copyright © 2018

Chapter One

"I'm telling you they're hot, Jessie. You don't know what you're missing until you've had two guys at one time. I hear the sex is explosive." Brenda, Jessica Winters' best friend, waved her hands in front of her face.

"Why would I want two men to have to pick up after when one is hard enough? Can you imagine just how tired you'd be if you hooked up with two of them? You'd spend all your time cooking and cleaning. Nope, not for me." Jessie shrugged her shoulders.

"The women I know swear by it. They say they're so pampered and pleasured that they don't know what to do with themselves when their men are at work. I'm telling you, getting into a relationship with a pair of the handsome hunks in this town would be like hitting the jackpot on double Tuesdays." Brenda wasn't giving up.

"If dating two men is so amazing, why aren't you doing it?" Jessie asked.

"Because I'm already in love with Tommy. Otherwise, I'd be all over a couple of them in a heartbeat."

"What happened to Riverbend while I was away the last few years getting my masters? All of a sudden there are five or six families made up of threesomes when I'd never heard of it before." Jessie stared at her menu.

The Pizza House was a new venue that one of those threesome families had opened a couple of months back, and it was always crowded. They had delicious pizzas, pasta, and sandwiches. It was no wonder they stayed packed.

"They're looking your way, girlfriend. You've caught their attention. Now all you have to do is reel them in."

"What are they, fish? I'm no fisherman, Brenda. What are you going to get?" Jessie changed the subject, ignoring her friend.

Ever since Brenda had gotten engaged to her boyfriend, she'd been determined to fix Jessie up. It was as if Brenda wanted her to be just as happy as she was. Well, she was happy. Okay, happy but lonely. Brenda spent a lot of her spare time with her new fiancé, which left Jessie on her own more than she was used to. Many of her old friends were either married and had a couple of kids or had moved away from Riverbend.

"You are coming out with us tomorrow night, right?" Brenda asked.

"I don't know. I need to work on lesson plans. School starts in two weeks," Jessie reminded her.

"So, what else do you have to do during the week? Work on them during the day and go out with us tomorrow night. You have to, Jessie. I need you to."

"Need me to? You've got Tommy. You don't need me."

"Sure I do. He only dances to slow music. I need someone to dance with when they're playing the good songs. Remember 'It's Raining Men'? We always dance to that one together."

"Fine. I'll go, but I'm not making any guarantees that I'll stay very late."

"Woohoo! We're going to have a blast." Brenda clapped her hands together.

Jessie narrowed her eyes at her friend. She had something up her sleeve. She was entirely too happy that Jessie was going out with them. With a sigh, Jessie resigned herself to being thrown at some poor man who wouldn't know what hit him. What were best friends for unless it was to set you up on a blind date you didn't even know you were going to have?

They ordered pizza, half cheese and hamburger and half pepperoni. They'd always liked to eat pizza, but rarely got it unless they went into one of the larger towns shopping. Riverbend was a small ranching community that was obviously growing. High on the growth factor seemed to be men who shared. Evidently the news had gotten out that they seemed to be accepted in the community, and it attracted more like-minded men.

"So, tell me about your teaching gig. Ae you excited?" Brenda asked.

"I am. I'll be teaching juniors English lit. I can't wait. I did a lot of student teaching in school, but now I'll be able to pick my own agenda and lessons." Jessie loved teaching and had gone back to school to get her masters so that she could teach high school English with the extra education under her belt.

"I can't imagine teaching. All those rowdy teenagers and grading papers. I'll stick with keeping books any day," Brenda said.

"See, keeping books sounds boring to me. We're just different people," Jessie said with a chuckle.

"I love it though. I like order, and bookkeeping is the epitome of order. Everything has to be in the right place for it to all come out right in the end," she said.

"So why were you at loose ends tonight instead of going out with your fiancé?" Jessie asked.

"He and his brothers are watching a ball game. I didn't want to hang around a bunch of men yelling and cursing. I'd much rather eat pizza with my bestie," Brenda said. Her face bloomed into a huge smile.

"I don't blame you. I'm glad you asked me, and this place is great. I'm glad it opened up, and it looks like it's going to get plenty of business so it stays open," Jessie said.

"Yeah, they're always busy at night and on the weekends. We should make this a regular hangout on Friday nights. Tommy and his brothers will probably keep watching games or playing poker on Friday nights. It's a great time for us to hang out." Brenda sat back when the waitress brought their pizza and set it in front of them.

"Sounds good to me. We've still got to go to Dallas or somewhere to shop for your dress, girlfriend. It won't be long before you'll be walking down that aisle," she told her friend.

"I know. Let's plan on next Saturday. I've been so busy with work lately that I haven't felt like shopping. And me not feeling like shopping is huge," Brenda pointed out.

"Are things settling down now that they've hired a full-time secretary?" Jessie asked.

"Yeah. Carmen is really nice. She's quiet though. Doesn't talk much about her past. I'm just glad they were able to get her. Trying to handle reception duties and my normal bookkeeping was really stretching me," Brenda said.

"Where did Carmen come from? I've never heard of her."

"She's from Austin. She moved here about two months ago and has been looking for a job. Not sure why she picked here to settle down, but it doesn't matter. She did, and I'm very happy about it."

They talked about Brenda's vision for her wedding and the type of wedding dress she wanted to look for as well as the bridesmaids' dresses. She'd already picked out the cakes that the local bakery would make for her. Jessie was beginning to get as excited for her friend as Brenda appeared to be.

She and Brenda had known each other all their lives. They'd been best friends for most of that time and had only been apart for the two years that Jessie had temporarily moved away to get her masters. Now that she was back, it was as if she'd never been gone.

"I can't wait until tomorrow night," Brenda said as they walked out to their respective cars. "We're going to have a blast. I just know it."

"As long as you don't have some blind date up your sleeve, I'll be happy. I'm not going there, Brenda. I hope you haven't planned anything like that."

"I haven't. I promise. I just want you to have a good time, that's all."

"I'm counting on it, girlfriend," Jessie said.

Jessie squeezed the other woman's hand and hugged her before leaving her at her car to walk over to her own. She loved Brenda like a sister, but the other woman was set on finding her a man. Jessie wasn't interested right now. She had her job to focus on. She couldn't wait to start teaching. She had only a few weeks to prepare and didn't have time to waste on a man. Or, as Brenda seemed to be pushing her toward, two men.

* * * *

"Wesson, hold her still while I check her back leg. She's holding it funny," Cole said.

He ran his hands down the horse's flank then traveled down her leg to feel for any abnormality he could find. His hand caught something stuck on the inside of her leg and sighed. It felt like a barb of some kind. Where had she picked up something like that?

"Found something on her inner leg. Try to keep her steady while I check it out," he said.

"What the hell would she be doing with something like that? We don't have any bushes like that around here," Cole said.

"Don't have a clue. Let me see what it looks like. At least it isn't a muscle strain we'd have to pen her up for."

Cole tried to see the spot while Wesson held the horse still, but he couldn't get a good visual. Instead he grasped the end of the barb and pulled it out with a quick jerk. Then he felt to see if the area would bleed. Nothing.

He scooted out from beneath the horse and stood to look at what he'd pulled out of the horse's upper leg. It looked like a dart of some kind. He held it up and turned it over and over. What the hell was it?

"Never seen anything like it before. Where in the hell did it come from?" Wesson asked.

"Don't have a clue what it is or how it got in her leg. Think we should call the sheriff and make out a report?" Cole asked.

"It's a one-off thing. Let's just see if it happens again."

"I don't like it. Someone is going around shooting these dart things. They're going to hurt someone or something more than this if they keep it up," he said.

"That's true. Maybe you're right and we should at least report it. They may even have had some other reports of this from one of the other ranches," Wesson said.

"We're lucky there wasn't anything on the dart that would have harmed the horse. It could have been dipped in poison or something." Cole didn't like that someone was going around with a dart gun of some kind.

"I'll call the sheriff and tell him what happened. Do you think we should keep Spice in the barn for a day or two to let her rest before letting her back out?" Cole asked.

"Yeah. Just to be sure she doesn't have any long-lasting effects. She'll probably be fine, but it won't hurt." Wesson sighed.

Cole watched as Wesson disappeared into the barn with the horse. The idea that there was someone out there using their horses for target practice grated on him. He wanted to find whoever it was and beat some sense into them. Even if they didn't have anything on them, they were dangerous to animals and people.

He walked inside the house he and his brother shared and headed straight for the office. He wondered if anyone else had reported finding darts in their horses or cattle. After taking a seat behind the desk, Cole punched in the number for the sheriff's department and leaned back to wait for someone to answer.

"Sheriff's office. This is Carol, how can I help you?"

"Hey, Carol. It's Cole Taylor at the Bar T Ranch. Is the sheriff available?" he asked.

"Just a minute, Cole. He just walked in but is on the other line," she said.

Cole waited for a good fifteen minutes before Sheriff Kinkade barked out an irritated, "Hello."

"Hey, sheriff, this is Cole out at the Bar T. We just found a dart on one of our horses. You get any other complaints like that recently?" he asked.

"Well, hell, Cole. This the first time it's happened? Haven't had any other calls like that."

"Yeah, first one we've found. Going to check over the rest of the cattle and horses, but that's going to take a hell of a lot of time to do."

He could hear the creak of the other man's chair as he leaned back in it. The sheriff was a good man and thorough when it came to doing his job.

"Got the dart?" he finally asked.

"Yeah. Not very big, but it could have had something on it and hurt or killed our horse," Cole pointed out.

"Keep it handy. When I'm out that way I'll pick it up. I'll have one of my deputies call around and see if anyone else has found one on their animals and just didn't report it," the sheriff said.

"Will do. Thanks." Cole ended the call and sat behind the desk thinking.

More than likely it was some bored teenager with nothing better to do. Kids needed activities to keep them busy so they didn't get into trouble like this. When he and Wesson had been kids, they'd had chores then jobs that kept them from getting themselves into trouble.

Well, mostly. They'd still managed to cause enough havoc that their pa had stepped in with a belt on occasion. He grinned at the memories. Yeah, his butt had hurt, but mostly it had been his pride that had taken the punishment. It wasn't that he and Wesson had gotten caught. It was that their pa had been disappointed in them. At the time they'd been misbehaving, it had seemed like fun.

He shook his head and sighed. He might as well get out there and start checking the rest of the horses then grab Wesson to start checking over the cattle. He didn't relish that job one bit.

Cole met Wesson at the corral and shared his conversation with the sheriff. His brother frowned but nodded.

"Guess we might as well get started. It's going to take most of the day. I'll radio the hands to start out where they are now. Hopefully between the five of us we can knock this out fairly quickly," Wesson said.

Cole sure as hell hoped so. He was looking forward to kicking back with a cold beer and listening to some music at the bar tonight. It had been a long week. Normally fall was a slow time for them. Just before winter kicked in, they had to watch the cattle closely for predators as well as keep them fed. Summer was spent keeping the watering holes clean and safe, and spring was foaling. What had happened to fall that they were just as busy as the rest of the year?

Cole followed his brother to the barn to saddle up their horses and get to work. Days like today he wished they had a woman to look forward to coming home to at the end of the day.

He and his brother had moved to Riverbend nearly three years ago, buying out an elderly couple who wanted to move closer to their children and grandchildren and get out of the ranching business. The place had needed a good bit of work since the old man hadn't been able to afford to keep it up like it needed to be. Now, they were proud of the ranch. It was running smoothly and was finally paying for itself.

Sure would be nice to find a nice woman who doesn't mind ranch life with all its ups and downs. I'd like a woman who could handle me and Wesson together. Surely there's one out there somewhere.

Cole climbed up on his horse and sighed. If other men had found their woman there in Riverbend, so could they. It might take some time, but eventually he was positive they'd find her.

Chapter Two

"God, this place is packed," Jessie nearly yelled to be heard over the music and loud voices all around them.

"It's Saturday night, hon. They're always busy on the weekends. The ranch hands are out kicking up their heels," Brenda pointed out.

"What do you gals want to drink?" Tommy asked.

"I'll have a Corona," Jessie said.

"Bud Light for me," Brenda said.

Tommy nodded and disappeared into the crowd. Jessie looked around at the crowded dance floor and wondered how Brenda expected them to dance with all the other people already spilling off the floor into the table areas.

"I don't remember this place ever being this busy before," she told Brenda.

"Town's growing. More people in town mean more people here. Not much else for entertainment other than the skating rink and bowling alley. That's where moms take the kids on Saturday afternoons before Saturday nights here."

"Do you remember going skating there on Friday nights?" Jessie asked.

"God, yes. We'd circle that floor for hours in hopes that one of the guys would notice us. I can still remember trying to breathe with the Spanx I wore to make my belly look flat," Brenda laughed.

"Don't make me remember that part. We were so stupid thinking we had to be skinny and blonde to attract one of the guys. Everything was so serious back then. Now I can look back and laugh at the trouble we went through."

Brenda grinned. "Remember summers laying out after suntan oil all over us to get a suntan? We'd plug in a fan and listen to the radio while we cooked under the sun."

"Cooked is right. I knew better, but still did it anyway and got sunburned every time." She sighed. "Those were good times, though."

"Here you go, ladies." Tommy returned with their beer. "Got lucky and a spot opened up at the bar right as I walked up. Otherwise I might have been waiting until they closed the joint down. Place is wild tonight."

They talked over the din around them about all the latest gossip and news. After about thirty minutes, Tommy pulled Brenda out on the crowded dance floor for a slow dance. She smiled at the happiness on her friend's face. Brenda was head over heels in love with Tommy, and he seemed just as in love with her. Jessie wanted to find that kind of love someday. The kind where you only had eyes for each other.

"Would you like to dance?" The deep voice startled her out of her thoughts.

It belonged to a tall dark-haired man with the most amazing light blue eyes she'd ever seen. They were so clear and bright she couldn't tear her eyes away from them.

"Excuse me?" she finally asked, shaking herself.

"I was wondering if you'd like to dance," he said.

"I'd love to, but I'm guarding drinks and the table." She hated that she would have to turn this guy down.

He was one seriously good-looking guy. His dark hair was shaggy, but not long. He had chiseled features with a strong chin and full lips she'd love to explore. His broad shoulders and wide chest narrowed down to a trim waist. He looked muscular, but not muscle bound like some men tended to be. More than likely his physique was due to hard work on a ranch instead of lifting weights at some club.

"No problem. I'll wait with you, and we'll take the next dance," he said, taking an empty chair that wasn't in front of a beer. "I'm Cole Taylor."

"Jessie Winters. Great to meet you, Cole."

Jessie hadn't seen him before as far as she could remember. He had to be one of the newly arrived crowd since she'd been gone. He was a welcome attraction as far as she was concerned. It surprised her that he'd opted to wait until she could dance rather than look for someone else. Most men would move on instead of sitting a dance out.

When the song ended, Tommy and Brenda returned, and Cole stood, holding out his hand to Tommy.

"Cole Taylor. I don't think I've met you before," he said.

"Tommy Jones, and this is my fiancée, Brenda. Nice to meet you." Tommy held Brenda's chair for her.

"Jessie wanted to wait until you guys returned before dancing with me. Hope you don't mind that I waited," he said.

Brenda spoke up before her fiancé could. "Not at all. Go dance." She waved them off.

Jessie shook her head with a smile at her friend's obvious attempt to push them together. Brenda would have them engaged and planning their wedding if Jessie knew her friend. It was just a dance. That was all.

"You've got the prettiest green eyes I've ever seen," Cole said once they'd claimed their postage stamp of a spot on the dance floor.

"Thank you." She didn't know what else to say.

"My brother and I own the Bar T Ranch north of town. Been here about three years. What do you do?" he asked.

They swayed to the song since they couldn't really move anywhere. It seemed much more intimate this way. She couldn't help but feel a little nervous at being so close to the man. He was a stranger to her, and they were pressed almost chest to chest.

"I'm a school teacher. I'm teaching juniors at the high school," she said.

"How do you like it?" he asked.

"Well, I haven't actually started, yet. I just got back in town a few months ago from getting my masters. I start in two weeks."

"Wow, a masters. That's serious education," he said.

"I wanted all the information I could get so I could teach college one day if I wanted to. The community college isn't that far away," Jessie said.

"I bet you're going to be a great teacher. Are you looking forward to it?" he asked.

"Can't wait to get started." She smiled up at him, enjoying the way he felt holding her.

It had been a long time since she'd felt a man's arms surrounding her. She'd dated a little bit while away at college, but none of it had been very serious, and none of them had affected her the way this man seemed to. She was super aware of his touch and the scent of leather aftershave, and something that must be his natural scent seemed to wrap its way around her body. She almost felt lightheaded with the heady aroma.

"So, do you raise horses or cattle?" she asked, looking up at him.

She couldn't get enough of staring into those amazing light blue eyes. They seemed to sparkle, and she loved it when he smiled and the corners of his eyes crinkled.

"Mostly cattle, but we do breed the occasional horse. Right now we're working to build up our stock though," Cole said.

"Do you like it here?" she asked.

"Love it. The town is growing, but still small enough that you've got good family morals and a laid-back atmosphere. We used to work a ranch right outside of Dallas, and the area seemed to be just as fast-paced as the big city. Didn't much like it. Once we were able to get up enough money to buy our own place, my brother and I looked for somewhere that would be different. We found that here in Riverbend," he said.

The song ended, and he walked her back to where Brenda and Tommy sat. He smiled down at her and thanked her for the dance.

"Maybe we could have another dance before the night is over," he said.

"Sure." She smiled up at him and felt her stomach flutter in anticipation of being in his arms again.

"So? Was he nice?" Brenda demanded as soon as Cole had walked out of earshot.

"Yeah. He's really nice. He and his brother own a ranch outside of town," she told her.

"Didn't think I recognized him," Tommy said.

"See, I told you that coming out tonight would be good for you. The way you're smiling I can tell you enjoyed the dance," Brenda pointed out with a smirk.

Jessie resisted rolling her eyes. There was no putting on the brakes with Brenda. She was going to push her toward the poor man the next chance she got.

Before Jessie could point out that it had only been one dance, another man walked up and smiled down at her. This one had warm brown hair and hazel eyes. He looked to be about six feet two inches and built just as fine as the last man had been. In fact, they looked a little alike. He smiled down at her.

"Would you like to dance?" he asked.

Jessie couldn't help but be flattered that two amazingly handsome men had asked her to dance before she'd even had time to drink her beer. She opened her mouth then closed it before finally answering him.

"Yes, I'd like that." Jessie let him help her to her feet then held his hand as they made their way through the throng to reach the dance floor.

For the second time in less than an hour Jessie found herself attracted to a man after only just meeting him. She leaned back slightly and looked up at him.

"My name's Jessie," she said.

"Sorry. That was rude of me. I'm Wesson. It's good to meet you, Jessie." He smiled down at her. "Very good to meet you."

She smothered the urge to giggle. She hadn't felt like giggling since she'd been a teenager. What was going on with her?

"You must be new to Riverbend. I haven't seen you before."

"Been here about three years now. Guess that could be considered new. My brother and I bought a ranch outside of town," he said.

Jessie nearly stopped dancing. Was this Cole's brother? What were the odds that she'd dance with both men back to back?

"Um, is Cole your brother?" she finally asked.

He smiled. "Yeah. You danced with him a few minutes ago."

"I see."

She wasn't sure she saw at all though. Why would both men want to dance with her?

"Said you were gorgeous, so I had to see for myself, and he wasn't lying. You are."

"Thank you. Do you usually dance with the same women your brother dances with?" she asked.

"Not all the time, but he was really taken with you. Had to meet you myself to see if he was crazy or not," he said.

"I guess it's a little crazy to me to realize that I've danced with two brothers in one night," she admitted.

"Don't let it bother you. Cole and I share everything. We're not in competition with each other," Wesson told her.

Jessie's mouth dropped open at his revelation. Shared everything? Did that mean they shared women? She closed her mouth and tried to think of something to say, but for the life of her, she couldn't come up with a single thing.

"I can tell I shocked you," he said. "I didn't mean to, but we don't hide how we feel about it."

"I know there are guys here in Riverbend who share, but I've never met any of them before. I guess it just shocked me to hear you say it," she admitted.

"That's okay. Does it bother you?" he asked.

She wasn't sure how to respond to that. Did it bother her? No. Not really. She could feel her face grow warm at his question and knew she was blushing. Damn her fair skin.

"It doesn't bother me, but I guess I am a little unsure about it all. It seems wrong to dance with both of you like this," she said.

"Why? We planned to both dance with you to get to know you. Nothing wrong with getting to know you, is there?" he asked.

"No, I guess not." She liked both men, and that bothered her.

The song ended, and Wesson walked her back to the table where her friend was waiting on her. Tommy was notably absent.

"Thanks for the dance, Jessie," he said, holding her chair for her.

She smiled up at him, unable to do anything else since she'd enjoyed it and liked him despite the fact she'd found his brother just as attractive and interesting.

"He looks hot, too. What did you think about him?" Brenda asked.

"He's nice. Um, he's the other guy's brother," she admitted.

Brenda covered her mouth with one hand and squealed. "They both danced with you? That's great. I bet they share. Did he say anything about it?"

"Yeah. He did. It feels kind of weird to have danced with two brothers like that," she said.

"What did he say?"

"That they shared everything and both wanted to get to know me."

"Oh. My. God. They're hitting on you."

"I don't think it's like that. We just met, Brenda." She looked around. "Where's Tommy?"

"Bathroom and to get us fresh beers." Brenda reached over and grasped her hand. "Do you like them?"

"Brenda. I just danced one dance with each of them. It's not like I got their life history or anything."

"Still. It's exciting. You've only been out this once and already have the attention of a couple of hot-looking men," Brenda said.

"You better not be talking about other men looking hot while I'm slaving away at the bar trying to get you another beer, woman." Tommy plopped the three bottles on the table and sat next to Brenda.

"I'm talking about hot men for Jessie. I have my own personal hot hunk of man right here," she said, leaning into him.

"Mind watching our drinks again? I want to dance," Brenda said, jumping up and dragging her fiancé up behind her.

"I've got them." Jessie smiled at the couple as they were swallowed up in the crowd.

"Mind if we join you while your friends are dancing?"

Jessie looked up to see both Cole and Wesson standing next to her. Separately they were amazing to look at. Together they were awe-inspiring with their good looks and the way their eyes brightened with their smiles. She could only nod as they sat down next to her.

"Do you ride?" Wesson asked her.

"Um, yeah. I haven't in several years, but I used to ride a lot when I was younger," she said.

"Would you like to go riding next weekend?" Cole asked.

"Next weekend?" She fought to keep up with them.

They were asking her out to go riding with them. Should she? There were two of them. Sure, there were other threesomes in town, but did she want to go down that path?

"Nothing serious," Wesson said. "Just a ride and maybe a picnic. We want to get to know you, Jessie."

"I don't know. I'm a little uncomfortable with going out with two men at one time," she admitted.

"Are you embarrassed about it?" Wesson asked, sitting back.

"No. Not embarrassed, just not sure how I feel about dating two men."

"Then go riding with us and decide that way. You can't make an informed decision without trying it out," Cole said.

She sighed and felt her mouth turn up in a small smile. They were right. Still, Jessie felt a little unsure. She drew in a deep breath and nodded.

"Okay. I'll go riding with you. Where exactly is your ranch? I'll drive out Saturday," she said. She'd have to cancel her trip with Brenda if she did.

They told her where they lived, and she instantly recognized the ranch as being the old Lazy S Ranch that the Smiths had owned when she was growing up.

"Plan on being there about nine, and we'll take a picnic lunch with us," Wesson told her.

"Sounds good," Jessie told them.

"Here come your friends," Cole said. "Dance with us now that they're back."

"With both of you?" she asked, her voice going higher at the idea of dancing in public with the two men.

"It's a fast song. Nothing wrong with the three of us dancing," Wesson said, drawing her to her feet.

"Um, Brenda, I'm going to dance. Watch my beer for me, okay?" Jessie asked.

"Don't worry. We're not going anywhere," Brenda said with a wide smile. "Have fun."

Jessie wasn't sure how she'd ended up going from a reluctant night out with Brenda and her fiancé to dancing with two hot guys at one time. Her life was proving to be anything but boring.

Chapter Three

Wesson watched as Jessie climbed out of her car and couldn't help but admire the way she filled out her jeans. The woman was built just like he liked a woman to be. All curves and softness that made his dick harden at just the sight of her. When she noticed him, she smiled and the day seemed to brighten even more.

"Hey there," she said, walking in his direction.

"Hey yourself. You look great. Ready for some riding?" he asked.

"Just remember it's been a while for me. No wild romps across the fields," she warned.

"Nope. No racing. I promise," he said, though wild romps made him think of other pleasures.

"Where's Cole?" she asked, looking around.

"Saddling up the horses. We've chosen Sugar for you. She's gentle and sure footed. You'll like her. She has a smooth gait," he said.

God the smile she gave him seemed to melt something inside of him. His shaft jerked in his pants, making him want to adjust it away from his zipper. Fuck she was hot.

"Thanks. I'm a little nervous about being on a horse after so many years. How far are we going before we stop to eat?" she asked.

"About two hours, but we'll break it up into one hour rides and stop for a walk break. Don't worry. We're not going to ruin you for future rides." He winked at her.

Cole walked out, leading two horses. Wesson couldn't help noticing that his brother's face lit up at the sight of Jessie. He'd talked non-stop about the woman all week. There was no doubt that his brother was already hooked on her. He just hoped she turned out to be the right woman for them. He was already thinking future with her, and that had never happened with any other woman before.

Usually he held back his enthusiasm to see how things went after a date or two, and when they didn't work out, he wasn't too upset over it. The fact that he already wanted her to be the one surprised him. If she walked away, he could already tell it would hurt.

"Hey, Cole."

Wesson watched as Jessie walked over to run her hand down the muzzle of one of the horses.

"You look great, Jessie," Cole said.

"Thanks. I can't wait to ride again. Wesson said I'm riding Sugar. Is one of these Sugar?" she asked.

"This is Sugar over here," Cole told her. He indicated the roan with a white muzzle.

Wesson smiled as Jessie walked over and rubbed her hand up and down the horse's face, talking to the horse like she would a beloved dog or cat. She obviously loved animals, which was always a plus in his book.

"Let me get my horse and we can get going," Cole said.

Wesson walked over to where Jessie was cooing to Sugar. "Let me help you up, babe."

He held his clasped hands to allow her to use them to mount Sugar. She climbed up like a pro and settled on the saddle taking the reins from him. She looked good, sitting up on the horse, like a natural. He couldn't help but admire her astride the big horse. Her posture was natural, and compounded with her amazing body, Wesson couldn't help but think of her astride his body, riding his cock.

Cole returned, riding his horse out of the barn. Wesson climbed up on Charger, and the three of them began the trip to the spot he and Cole had picked out to have their picnic.

"So what have you been doing all week?" Wesson asked as they rode.

"Lesson plans mostly. I did manage to clean out the flower bed though. The weeds were about to take over," Jessie said.

"So school starts for you in another week, right?" Cole asked.

"Yeah. We'll go the first week with the kids coming in on Friday to get their schedules and learn their teachers before they break for Labor Day. After that, they'll come back on Tuesday full time." Jessie shook her head. "The first couple of weeks is tough for them and for us getting back into the rhythm. The kids don't want to be there but finally relax by the third week."

"What about you? Do you really enjoy teaching?" Wesson asked.

"Love it. I love it when they get interested in a story or book for the first time and love hearing them discuss one among themselves. They come up with some of the craziest ideas about what the author was trying to get across in the story," she said.

"You must really like the classics to teach them," Cole said. "What about current authors?"

"Oh, don't get me wrong. I love reading romance books. I have a huge selection on my e-reader." She grinned back at Cole over her shoulder.

"Romance, huh? Like dirty romance?" Wesson asked.

He could just imagine her curled up reading a dirty ménage book. He'd heard all about some of those from some of the guy friends they had who had wives that read them. It seemed that they got the best sex after their women had been reading one.

He smiled at her quick intake of breath. He'd caught her off guard with that statement.

"Well, they are pretty hot," she finally admitted.

He just bet they were. Their Jessie had a penchant for dirty books. That meant she might not be against letting his brother and him spend more time with her. He sure as hell hoped so. Just the fact that she'd agreed to go riding with both of them had given him hope. Hope he hung on to with both hands.

* * * *

Jessie shivered at the thoughts racing through her head. She couldn't believe she'd admitted to reading hot romance to them. What had she been thinking? Well, she hadn't. All that had consumed her mind for the last hour had been how good the men had looked in their blue jeans and button-down western shirts that had accented their wide shoulders and broad chests. Chests she had an itch to explore. What was wrong with her?

They stopped next to a circle of rocks where Cole helped her down while Wesson tethered the horses to some tree limbs.

"Thought you could use a few minutes to walk around and stretch your legs," Wesson said as he returned to where she and Cole stood.

"Thanks. I definitely could use a quick walk. I'm going to be sore tomorrow," she told him.

"Just soak in a hot tub with some Epsom salts tonight, and you shouldn't be too sore tomorrow. We'll have to do this regularly so you get used to riding again," Wesson said.

Regularly? It sounded like they wanted to spend more time with her, and they hadn't even been around each other for more than a few hours, including the night they'd danced with her. She couldn't stop her heart from stuttering at the thought of dating them both. Could she do it? Could she go out with two men at one time on a regular basis? Jessie really wasn't sure. She knew one thing though. If she planned to go out at all, it would have to be with both of them. She couldn't choose one over the other one. She wasn't even sure they'd go out with her without the other one.

From the beginning they'd made it clear that they shared. Jessie couldn't pretend otherwise. If she decided to spend more time with them, she had to decide if she could handle that. Hell, she should have made up her mind before coming on this riding trip with them. It wasn't fair that she agreed to the picnic when she hadn't really made up her mind about the long term should they still be interested after this.

I'm such an idiot. I like both of them. I could never choose, so either I date them both or I let them go after today.

The problem was she didn't want to let them go. She already liked them both too much to put an end to their relationship. But what about dating both of them and teaching at the same time? Would her seeing two men at one time affect her position with the school? Were there other teachers in ménage relationships in Riverbend?

Jessie needed to find out but wasn't sure how to do it. She'd talk to Brenda about it. No doubt the woman would be ecstatic once she found out that Jessie was possibly getting serious about Cole and Wesson. She'd have to be damn sure she really was before she approached her friend. There'd be no stopping the other woman. She'd be planning a wedding right alongside her own.

I need to cool it. This is just a first date and doesn't mean we'll ever see each other again. I'm getting ahead of myself.

Still, the worry that she'd have trouble with her job nagged at her as she stretched her legs while the guys waited on her.

"How are you doing? Feel like heading out again?" Cole asked her.

She smiled and nodded. "I'm good."

Cole helped her up, and then the three of them started off again. She had to admit that the views were amazing as they wound their way around rocks and jutting trees. Jessie would never have seen the serene scenery had she not accepted their date.

The rest of the ride was made in near silence with the guys breaking it here and there to point out jackrabbits or the occasional roadrunner. Once they reached a grassy meadow she slipped off Sugar with Wesson helping her down before Cole walked the horses over to a stream to drink before tethering them to a scrub tree.

"It's beautiful here," she breathed out.

"We like coming here when we're feeling fenced in with work," Wesson admitted.

"The stream looks inviting. I just might need to peel off these boots and my socks and soak my feet in it," she said.

"That's a great idea. Why don't you do that while we set up the blanket and food," Cole suggested.

"Really? I don't mind helping," she said.

"We've got it covered. You go soak your toes," Wesson said.

Jessie didn't wait to see if they were teasing or not. She strode over to the stream and shucked her boots, socks, and rolled up her pant legs before dipping her feet in the warm stream. It felt amazing. She carefully walked around before settling on a rock with her feet submerged in the water. Leaning back on her hands, she lifted her face up to the warm sunshine and enjoyed the freedom she felt just sitting there.

After a while, she pulled her feet from the water to let them dry before she had to pull on her socks and shoes again. Ten minutes later, Wesson nudged her with his shoulder.

"Ready to eat?" he asked.

She opened her eyes, unable to contain her wide smile. "Yeah. This is an amazing spot to just relax. I can see why you and Cole come here sometimes to unwind."

"Hey, Cole. Come get her boots and socks," Wesson said.

Before she realized what he was going to do, he'd picked her up and carried her over to the blanket they'd spread out in the sparse shade of one of the small scrub trees.

"I could have walked," she complained with a frown.

"Why walk when you had me to carry you? Besides, your feet aren't completely dry. You'd have gotten them dirty and possibly bruised from the rocks," Wesson told her.

She sighed. He was right. Still, being in his arms had been disconcerting. She was very aware of her plus-sized body and worried that he'd hurt himself trying to carry her. She watched him closely for any sign that she'd done just that. He didn't act the least winded or like he'd strained his back.

"Okay, we've got ham and cheese sandwiches, potato salad, chips, and brownies," Cole announced, setting her boots and socks to one side of the blanket.

"Sounds yummy," she told them.

The two men set out the food, passing her a full plate before getting their own. Wesson poured sweet tea from a thermos in three plastic cups, and they all dug in.

"This is really good potato salad. Who made it?" she asked.

"That would be Cole. He's the cook between us. I burn water," Wesson admitted with a lopsided grin.

Jessie laughed. "I'm decent, but not great. I have about four or five meals I can cook with any luck. Much more than that, and I'm lost."

"Wesson isn't allowed in the kitchen unless it's to make sandwiches," Cole said with a low chuckle. "He nearly burned the house down once when he tried to scramble eggs."

"Did not. I put out the fire before it even managed to hurt the stove." Wesson threw a small pebble at his brother.

"Regardless, I made the potato salad, and he helped put the sandwiches together. I have to admit that the brownies came from the bakery in town. I got them yesterday. I suck at desserts," Cole said.

"It's all good. Thanks for inviting me, guys. I've really enjoyed this." Jessie smiled and leaned back on the blanket after finishing her brownie. "I'm full."

"Let us clean this up, and then we can lie back and watch the clouds. Bet I can pick out some cloud animals," Cole said.

"I haven't watched clouds since I was a teenager," Jessie admitted.

She watched as the two men quickly put away the food, and then the three of them stretched out on the blanket and relaxed.

"See over there? That's a teddy bear," Wesson said, pointing to her left.

Try as she might, Jessie couldn't see it. She just laughed and shook her head. "Your teddy bear doesn't look like any bear I've seen before."

"There," Cole said, pointing directly overhead. "That's a duck. See the bill on it?"

"I can just make it out. I think the clouds are moving too fast to play this game," she suggested.

Cole looked over at her. "You're probably right. I'm so full I think I'll just take a quick nap."

"Sounds good to me, too," Wesson said.

Jessie yawned as if their words had pulled it from her. A nap sounded good. It spoke volumes that she was able to settle down to close her eyes while situated between two very handsome, very virial men. She trusted them and felt safe falling asleep between them.

Chapter Four

Jessie felt something tickle her nose. She swiped at it then rubbed her nose. It brushed against her nose again. This time she frowned and opened her eyes to find Wesson bent over her with a flower between his fingers.

"Wake up, sleepyhead. It's time to get up."

She yawned and stretched. "How long was I asleep?"

"About an hour. Cole and I just woke up, as well." He bent over, and before she knew what he was going to do, Wesson kissed her lightly on the lips.

The quick kiss sent tiny butterflies flittering in her stomach. It was such a brief touch of his lips that she was surprised at the reaction it elicited. Was she really that attracted to him that one innocent kiss would stir her up like that? She barely knew him.

Than Cole reached down and helped her to her feet. Instead of letting her hand go, though, he pulled her in close to him, threaded his fingers into her hair close to her scalp, and brushed his mouth across hers in a slightly longer kiss. Again those damn butterflies flitted around in her belly.

"You look sweet when you're sleeping. And you've got the cutest little snore," Cole teased.

"I don't snore," she claimed, slapping her hands on her hips.

"Sure you don't, babe," Wesson told her.

"Really, you guys are just teasing me," she accused.

"Ready to mount up and head back?" Cole asked.

She huffed out a breath and nodded. "I've loved this. It's been wonderful. I almost hate to leave." She reluctantly pulled her socks and shoes back on.

"We can do it again anytime you want to, sweet thing," Cole said. "We've enjoyed it, too."

When Cole helped her up on Sugar once more, Jessie swore he kept his hand on her leg a little longer than was necessary. Were they as attracted to her as she was to them? Their kisses had stirred up feelings she'd never had before. Warmth had spread all the way to her toes. She needed to think about this once she wasn't in their company. She couldn't think with them so close to her. Was she seriously considering seeing them again?

Well, yeah. She shouldn't have come with them in the first place if she wasn't serious about possibly having a relationship with them. It was insane, but she truly liked both of them.

I'm crazy, but I really do want to get to know them both. Even though I know they share.

Jessie chatted with them about their ranch and her years at school all the way back to the ranch. When Wesson helped her down, she slid down his body and felt his long, hard erection pressed against her ass as she did. He didn't let her go, either. Instead he turned her around to face him and wrapped his arms loosely around her as she stood there.

"We really enjoyed today, Jessie," he said.

She felt Cole's warm breath at the back of her neck. His body pressed against her from behind.

"We want to see you again. I know you're getting ready to go back to work, but maybe you'd let me cook you supper Friday night?" Cole asked.

"Um, I…" she began.

"That will give you the rest of the weekend to get ready," Wesson pointed out.

"Um, okay. That sounds nice. I'd like that," she finally got out.

A second date meant she was seriously considering them for more than a one-off thing. Jessie prayed she wasn't making a mistake.

"Great. Plan to come over around five and we can talk some before we eat," Cole told her.

"Sounds great."

The next thing she knew, Wesson was pulling her in close to him. His head dipped, and his mouth slanted over hers, his teeth nibbling at her lower lip. She opened to him and allowed him entry. His tongue tangled with hers before he slowly pulled back and kissed the tip of her nose. He turned her around, and Cole pulled her into his arms. Only his kiss was gentle and soft, coaxing her mouth to open for him, where Wesson had demanded it from her.

When Cole pulled back, he brushed another light kiss across her lips then stepped back. "I'll walk you to your car."

Jessie allowed him to open her car door for her. He leaned in and kissed her once more before closing the door for her.

Both men waved as she drove down the long drive leading to the road back to town. Jessie wasn't sure what had just happened, but she felt as if they'd made a promise to her that they weren't going to let her go now that they'd spent time with her. Somehow she didn't mind that one bit.

* * * *

"Hey, Brenda. How are you doing?" Jessie asked the next day after calling her best friend on the phone.

"Great. How did your date go yesterday?" she asked.

Jessie was supposed to have called her when she got home and tell her all about her time with Wesson and Cole but had decided to wait until she'd slept and mulled it over in her head before she called the other woman.

"Really good. I had a great time. We rode out to where there's a stream and had a picnic beside it. It was great," she admitted.

"Sounds like you really did enjoy it. Why didn't you call me last night, huh? Did you spend a little more time than that with them?" Brenda asked, her voice very suggestive.

"No. I was home by five. I just needed to think about things before I called you. They asked me to have dinner with them at their place on Friday. That was going to be our night out, but I thought maybe you wouldn't mind if I took a raincheck on it."

"Hell, no. Of course you have to go with them. So they can cook?" Brenda asked.

"Well, Cole can, but Wesson is banned from the kitchen according to them," Jessie said with a laugh.

Brenda chuckled. "Well, as long as one of them can cook a decent meal you've got a good thing going with them. So you're going to see them again. That must mean you're attracted to them."

"That's what I kind of wanted to talk to you about. I'm worried about how it will affect my job, Brenda. I am attracted to them but don't want to get serious if it's going to be a problem with school. Do you know if any of the teachers are in a threesome?" Jessie asked.

"No. But one of the ladies on the school board is. I really don't think it will be an issue, Jessie," Brenda said.

Jessie nibbled her lower lip. She had hoped there would be another teacher, but a member of the board was better than nothing. Should she continue dating the two men, she was afraid it would come up at some point.

"I hope you're right. I really like them, Brenda. I never thought I would consider dating more than one man at the same time, but they're both really nice."

"Not to mention they're awesome to look at," Brenda pointed out with a laugh.

"There is that."

"Go for it, girl. You deserve to be happy. No one should be able to dictate who you can and can't see," Brenda said.

"Well, if you're sure you don't mind putting off our night out, I'm going to have dinner with them Friday night. I suppose I'll see if I'm still as interested in them then as I am now. There's just something about how different from each other they are. Wesson is more aggressive while Cole is laid back and teasing."

"Wesson isn't rough with you, is he?" Brenda asked with a hint of alarm in her voice.

"No. I just mean he does and says what he wants to without trying to filter his thoughts. He isn't in the least abrasive or rude. I would never tolerate that. You know that, Brenda."

"Just so he doesn't push you into anything you don't really want, Jessie." Brenda's words warmed her. Her friend was only looking out for her.

"Don't worry. I won't let them take advantage of me or anything. I really don't think they're like that at all."

"Good. Maybe we can have brunch Sunday after your date Friday night and talk for a while before you have to hurry off to get ready for school on Monday," Brenda suggested.

"Sounds like a plan. I'll talk to you later," Jessie said then ended the call.

She'd had a wonderful time with the guys the day before, and the more she thought about it, the more she knew she wanted to see where things went from there. Jessie had dreamed about them. They'd been by the stream lying on the blanket when suddenly they were all naked, writhing together in the moonlight. She'd felt totally cared for by the way both men kissed and caressed her body at the same time. It had been amazing despite it only being a dream. She'd woken before anything more had happened, and she had to admit that she'd been a little disappointed to have missed out on the main event.

* * * *

Cole started picking up the dishes from breakfast with Wesson putting away the butter and milk. They'd eaten in silence, but Cole knew they were each thinking about Jessie. H knew he sure as hell was. All he could think about was her. The erotic dream he'd had that night had been mind-blowing. She was every bit as delicious as he'd imagined when he'd first caught sight of her in the pizza place then again at the bar.

I can't get my mind off her. I've never obsessed over a woman like I am Jessie.

Thinking about her had his dick stiff and his balls aching. He wanted to make love to her so badly he groaned as his cock pressed against the cabinet while he washed dishes.

Wesson stood next to him drying the dishes and putting them away. From the way he walked, Cole figured his brother was having his own problems.

"Did you dream about her last night?" Cole finally asked.

"Hell, yeah. Dreamed I was balls deep inside of her and you were getting your cock sucked at the same time. Not sure how I feel about dreaming about your cock, brother.

Cole laughed. "About the same as I felt having you in my dream. I guess it just proves we were always going to share a woman."

"She's something else, man."

"I know. I'm so into her I can't think straight."

Wesson sighed. "Do you think she'll last?"

"I sure as hell hope so. She could be the one."

"Yeah. I was thinking the same thing. I can't stop fantasizing about her."

"I sure as hell enjoyed that kiss," Cole said. "The only bad thing about it was how quick it was, but I was afraid of spooking her."

"Me, too. Having both of us all over her would probably scare her off right now. We've got to take it slow and lure her into caring about us too deeply to run away."

"I agree," Cole said.

"Don't you just love all that rich brown hair and how it curls at the ends?" Wesson asked.

"Yeah, she's got the prettiest brown eyes. They got all warm and liquid looking when we kissed her," Cole said.

"And that body. Fuck me, Cole, she's got a rocking body. Just enough tits to fit in our hands and an ass that's plump and grabbable. I want to bury my face in her soft belly and lick her all over," Wesson said.

"She's perfect for us. She fits between us like she was made for us."

"We can't come on too strong, Cole. She'll run for sure. I'm surprised she agreed to have dinner with us. I know she's worried about dating two men at one time. She was uncomfortable dancing with us at the bar."

"We need to take her out to town next time to get her used to being out in public with us. I don't want her to feel embarrassed or uncomfortable being with us. If all we do is see her around here, she's going to balk the first time someone looks at her wrong."

Cole knew his brother was right. If she never got used to being with them in public, their relationship was doomed before it even got started.

"Let's take her to the steak house the first time she's available. She's going to be busy with school, but she ought to be able to go out to eat Saturday night," Wesson suggested.

"I agree. Maybe we can call a few of the guys we've met and ask them to all go out at the same time so she can see other threesomes out in public while we're there," Cole said.

"I bet Justin and Paul would love to take their Lana out. Then there's Randy, Travis, and Angela. They're all bound to welcome a little alone time with their women. They can get a babysitter for their kids and spend a nice dinner with each other." Wesson nodded.

Cole would call them and make the suggestion. He was sure he could enlist their help with their courtship of Jessie. They'd all had the same issues with convincing their women that loving two men at one time didn't have to be an issue for them.

"I'd give them a call tonight. It will give them time to locate a babysitter," Wesson said.

"I will. Maybe this will help convince her that seeing both of us isn't really an issue here in Riverbend."

"I sure hope so. I really like her. I mean *really* like her." Wesson ran a hand through his hair and shook his head. "Fuck me. If she decides she can't handle a threesome, I'm not going to take it very well."

Cole was surprised his brother had fallen this far so soon. Normally he was the one to hold back. It was just another sign that Jessie could be the one for them.

Chapter Five

Jessie sat at a booth with Brenda waiting on Angela, who was married to Randy and Travis, ranchers in Riverbend. She was nervous but did her best to hide it. It had been Brenda's idea to meet one of the women in town who was in a ménage relationship.

"Honey, you can't make an informed decision about giving those two a chance if you don't hear more about it. Angela is a sweet girl. She's head over heels in love with her men, too." Brenda patted Jessie's arm.

A pretty woman hurried over to their table and pulled Brenda into a hug. "It's so good to see you again. Sorry I'm late."

Brenda smiled up at her. "Have a seat. This is Jessie, Jessie, Angela Woods."

Jessie couldn't help but like the other woman with the huge smile on her face and the twinkling in her eyes. She truly did look happy. Was that happiness because of her men?

"It's great to meet you, Jessie. Don't you just love Riverbend? I'm basically new here. I've only been in town for about three years now. Best thing that ever happened to me," she said, beaming at them.

"You look especially happy right now. You're glowing, Angela. What's up?" Brenda asked her.

"I'm pregnant! I just told the guys last night. I'm so excited," she gushed out.

"Congratulations, Angela. That's great news. I know Randy and Travis are happy," Brenda said.

"To say the least. I didn't think they were going to let me come to town alone today. They're going to drive me insane. I can already tell." Angela took a sip of water then turned her attention to Jessie. "So, Brenda tells me that you're dating Wesson and Cole. They're really nice men."

"They are. I'm just not sure about going out with both men. I mean it's not a normal relationship. Aren't their problems being with two men?" Jessie asked.

"Well, not the kind you'd expect. There isn't any jealousy or rivalry. Mostly it's trying to balance their combined need to take care of me and protect me. They get bossy at times when they think I'm doing too much or something, but I wouldn't give them up for the world. They complete me in ways I can't even begin to explain," Angela told her.

"What about going out in public? Isn't it uncomfortable?" Jessie asked her.

"Not really. There are several other ménage relationships in Riverbend, and even the sheriff is in one. You don't have to worry about that." Angela waved her hand. "Sure, there are a few people in town who don't approve, but for the most part, everyone pretty much accepts us. Now that there are so many, we should really get a group of the woman together every once in a while and go out for dinner and drinks. It would be fun."

Brenda laughed. "That would sure be a wild group. Do you think you gals could get your men to allow it without them around to watch over you?"

"You've got a point. Maybe if we have it at the pizza place they won't complain too much," Angela said.

"Maybe," Brenda laughed out. "All I know is that they keep their eyes on you all the time when you're out in public."

"Maybe I'm not cut out for this. I don't know if I could handle someone constantly monitoring my every move. That sounds smothering to me," Jessie said.

"It's not as bad as it sounds. They don't really follow you around or anything. We're making it sound a lot worse than it is. I just want you to realize how much they care about their women and how much they want to keep them safe and happy. Don't not give them a chance because you're afraid they'll hover over you. It's not like that." Angela sighed. "I'm not helping much, am I?"

"I'm supposed to go to their house this weekend for dinner. I'll see how they are there before I make up my mind. I don't want things to go too far before I decide to call it off or if I can give this a try."

"Just remember that they will never fight over you or around you about anything. If they're having a disagreement, they'll settle it between themselves. They won't involve you. That's why ménage relationships works so well," Angela told her.

"And you're really happy with two men?" Jessie asked, narrowing her eyes.

"Ecstatically. The sex is explosive, and nothing compares to having two men to cuddle with on the couch watching TV or in bed on a cold winter's night." Angela grinned as the waitress brought their drinks out.

Jessie listened to Angela and Brenda catch up on the town's gossip. She couldn't help but admire the young woman. She was living with two men and was pregnant carrying their child. She didn't have a clue whose it was, and evidently, she didn't care. According to her, the men didn't care either. It all boggled Jessie's mind.

They ordered their meals and continued talking for another hour before Jessie excused herself to return home. She thanked Angela for agreeing to meet with them and tell her about what went into a ménage relationship then returned home to finish up the school work she was setting up for next week when school started.

Despite trying to concentrate on lesson plans, written exercises, and homework questions, Jessie kept thinking about her upcoming date with the guys. How could two brothers, who were similar in some ways but very different in others, share a woman between them without getting jealous at some point or another? Would she sleep with one every other night, or would they always sleep together? Who did she make love with on what day?

She felt heat burn from her neck up to her cheeks at the hints Angela had thrown about anal sex and taking both men at one time. She fanned her cheeks with one hand and grabbed her glass of iced tea with the other. Could she handle both men at one time? Was it really possible?

Well, evidently it was since Angela had talked about it. Still, the thought of those two men filling her at the same time was a bit scary. Though she hadn't seen them in the flesh, she'd felt their hard lengths against her body when they'd brushed up against her. They were much larger than any other man she'd ever been with in the past.

I can't keep thinking about this. I'm never going to get ready for school if all I think about is sex with Wesson and Cole.

But it was all she could think about. Even when she laid down to sleep that night, her mind whirled with thoughts of the two men. She'd loved how attentive they'd been while they'd been riding and on the picnic. They'd been perfect gentlemen for the most part. Only kissing her and never pushing her to go further. How would they be once they decided it was time to take the next step? Would that be this weekend?

Do I want it to be this weekend?

Truthfully, Jessie wasn't sure. All she could do was wait and see how everything went once that day came. Until then, she desperately needed some sleep.

When it came, it was filled with Wesson's and Cole's hands on her body, making her want, need. They made love to her with fiery kisses and smoldering looks as they caressed her body with their hands and lips. Jessie was consumed by them and had made up her mind about them in those heated dreams and didn't even know it.

* * * *

"I wish you would have let us pick you up, babe," Wesson said as he opened the door to her Friday night.

Jessie smiled up at him when he pulled her in for a warm hug. "There's no need to make extra trips into town when I can drive. But thanks again for the offer."

He brushed her lips with a soft kiss then led her into the living room where a large leather sofa in a warm chocolate brown stood in front of a stone fireplace. There were two burnt-orange leather recliners to one side in front of a flat screen TV and various end tables scattered around.

Jessie was relieved to see that there weren't any animal heads or horns adorning the walls. Though she wasn't totally against hunting, she didn't like the idea of dead animals staring at her all the time.

"How has your week been?" Wesson asked as he led her through the overly large living area.

"Productive. I got pretty much everything I needed to do finished for school. Now it's just getting settled into my classroom and setting everything up for when the kids start," she said.

They walked into the kitchen that was separated from the living area by an island on one side. She instantly fell in love with the black appliances and marble countertop. The warm oranges and yellows in the backsplash and tiled floors gave the room a homey appearance.

"I love the house, guys. It's amazing. You had to have completely redone it. I know it wasn't like this when you moved in," she said.

Cole chuckled. "Yeah, it took some time, but we got it like we want it. Even updated the master bathroom last year."

"I'll give you a complete tour after dinner if you want it," Wesson offered. "I think dinner is about ready."

"I can't wait. It smells Italian," she said, lifting her nose in the air.

"Lasagna," Cole said with a huge grin.

"Yummy. I love lasagna. And you made it yourself?" she asked.

"Yep. All by myself." Cole sighed when Wesson cleared his throat. "I had a little help from Wesson. He cut up the vegetables and made the salad."

"I'm impressed. Good thing you kept him away from the actual cooking part if he can't boil water," she teased, knocking her shoulder against Wesson's.

"Have a seat, Jessie. I'll bring it over to the table," Cole said. "Wesson, get the salad out of the fridge."

They spent the next hour eating and chatting about their week out working the ranch. Wesson entertained her with stories about their childhood while Cole added his version when Wesson made it sound like Cole had been the culprit in most of their pranks.

Jessie found herself having a wonderful time and really enjoyed the men's attentions. They touched her often. Just a light touch of their fingers to her arm or a casual caress at her elbow. It made her feel cared for, important to them. She could easily see herself falling for these men fast and hard. The big question was, could she handle two men at one time, all the time?

Questions swirled in her head about how it would work. Would they overwhelm her with there being two of them surrounding her all the time? She realized, though, once they were settled on the couch in the living room that she wanted to see where it took them. She wanted to give a threesome with these men a chance.

"Oh, I nearly forgot to tell you." Cole began looking over at Wesson. "The sheriff called while you were in the shower. Said they'd had another episode of one of the other ranchers finding darts in some of his cows. None of them were harmed, but that's three separate episodes. Got to be kids out target practicing or something."

"He needs to get to the bottom of it before someone gets hurt. It won't be long before they start upping the stakes. They're going to get tired of sitting targets and want to try something a little more challenging," Wesson said.

"Darts? What's going on?" Jessie asked, looking from one man to the other.

"Someone has been shooting darts at the horses and cows around the area. We found one in one of our horses last week. We're just lucky they aren't dipped in poison or something else. The horse wasn't really harmed," Cole told her.

"We think it's probably teenagers out getting their kicks, but it's a dangerous way to do that. They need to be caught and stopped before someone gets hurt," Wesson said.

"Do they sell guns that shoot darts in town?" she asked.

"Not that we know of. The sheriff is researching where they might have gotten the gun. In the meantime, we're keeping our eyes open. As long as they don't add poison or some drug to the tips, it's essentially harmless, but someone could get seriously hurt if they hit them in the face or neck." Cole shook his head. "Let's talk about something else now."

Jessie smiled. "Like what?"

"Like how beautiful you look in that green blouse. It matches your eyes and makes them sparkle," Cole told her.

She smiled up at him then felt Wesson's fingers at her neck, brushing aside her hair before kissing her at the juncture of her shoulder and neck. She couldn't stop the shiver that raced over her at the touch of his lips against her skin.

Cole leaned over and brushed a kiss against the corner of her mouth before cupping her cheek in one large, calloused hand and turning her to face him.

"I'm going to kiss you, Jessie. Say no if you don't want that," Cole said.

Jessie remained quiet. She wanted that kiss just as much as she wanted their hands on her body. Somewhere during the time they were eating and talking, Jessie had made up her mind that she wanted to find out where things would take them if she just let go. They were charming but firm in their beliefs and didn't appear to be afraid of hard work. They'd built the ranch back into a working entity that they could be proud of. Jessie wanted to know where their budding relationship might take them.

Slowly Cole lowered his head and pressed his lips against hers. He added the slightest amount of pressure until she opened her mouth to his. He didn't waste time after that. His tongue slipped inside and ravished her mouth, drinking from her low cries as he devoured her from the inside out.

Heat poured into her from their hands as they touched and caressed every part of her body through her clothes. She desperately wanted out of them to see what the heat from their caresses would feel like. How could she feel this way after only a couple of dates?

Cole's mouth released hers, and she felt herself turned toward Wesson as Cole nipped at her shoulder just below her neck. Wesson didn't brush lightly over her lips. He covered hers with a needy pressure that had her opening to him immediately. He built the need for more with the way he took her mouth with his, demanding her acceptance of his tongue tangling with hers as he took everything she could give with that one kiss.

When he released her, Jessie was gasping for breath, burning up with arousal, and certain that she was going to combust with even one more touch from them. Even as her head swam, they continued to kiss her, their mouths at her neck, her jaw, and the curve of her shoulder. Jessie could only moan at the mirrored exploration as they devoured her between them.

"Oh, God," she finally managed to get out.

"What do you need?" Wesson asked her. "Just tell us what you need, babe."

"I'm burning up," she whispered. "So hot."

"Let's get you out of those clothes then," Cole said.

She couldn't think with how they were touching her. She could only nod before they pulled her shirt over her head then removed her shoes and jeans. They left her underwear on as if giving her that one little piece of modesty while they explored her body with their hands and mouths.

"You taste so good, sweet darling," Wesson said. "I could eat you up."

They stretched her out on the couch and knelt next to her, loving on her as she writhed between them. They were killing her with their soft touches then the urgent feel of their mouths at her skin and through the lace of her underwear.

Wesson sucked at her nipple through the material of her bra He nipped at it then sucked again. When he moved to the other nipple, she felt Cole move one of her legs off the couch before settling between her legs and kissing down her abdomen to where her pussy was soaking her panties from their touches and kisses.

She tried to close her legs when he blew across the wet material, but with him lodged there, she couldn't do it. Heat burned her cheeks that he would see how wet she was.

"Be still, little wild cat. I'm going to taste you. You're soaking wet down here. Your little pussy is wet for us," Cole said.

She moaned when she felt his tongue through the material of her panties. He lapped at her with his hands against her inner thighs burning her skin there. She wanted more. She wanted them naked with her, letting her explore their amazing bodies, as well. Jessie opened her mouth to tell them but could only gasp when Wesson bit at one nipple as he pinched the other one through her bra.

"God how I want you," Wesson rasped out. "You're so damn responsive."

"Please," she managed to get out.

"What do you want, babe?" Wesson asked.

"I want you naked. I want to touch both of you like you're touching me," she told him.

"If we get undressed, Jessie, we aren't going to be able to stop until we've had you between us," Wesson said.

"I don't care. I need you. Need you both." Jessie squirmed, looking up at him, pleading with her eyes for him to agree.

"We need to move this to the bedroom," Cole said, standing from between her legs.

Wesson reached out and pulled Jessie to a sitting position then helped her stand. Her legs nearly buckled before Cole caught her and swung her up into his arms.

"Bring her clothes, Wesson." Cole carried her from the living room, down the hall to the bedroom.

The room was large and decorated in warm earth tones. There were no personal touches in this room. It looked like it wasn't used by either brother. Wesson deposited her clothes on a chair then turned down the covers to the bed before Cole gently laid her on the mattress. The expression on his face was of pure unadulterated need. It burned in his eyes as he stared down at her.

"You are so damn beautiful, Jessie. It almost hurts to look at you. Your skin is flushed and almost hot to the touch. Your eyes are darker green, and your lips are swollen from our kisses. I could look at you all day," Cole told her.

All she could do was moan. The need they'd built inside of her was almost too much to bear. She needed them, not their pretty words, right now.

"Touch me, Cole. I want to feel your hands on me. I want you both naked so I can touch you."

Wesson was already stripping before she had the words out of her mouth. Cole smiled down and slowly unbuttoned his shirt and slipped it from his shoulders, letting it fall to his feet while she watched. Then he slowly unfastened his belt buckle, followed by the button on his jeans, and slid the zipper down. He stopped there and pulled off his boots before pushing at his jeans until they were over his hips and down his legs where he stepped out of them.

Jessie's mouth watered at the sight of his tented boxers. There was a stain where his pre-cum had leaked from his obviously aroused cock. The sight of it made her mouth water. She wanted to taste them both. Wesson climbed on the bed as Cole shoved his boxers off and joined him on the other side of her.

Both men stretched out on the bed to suck and kiss at her skin from her neck down to her breasts. They each held a breast in one hand and molded it before devouring her nipples in their mouths. Each tug of their mouths had shards of pleasure searing her all the way to her clit. She squirmed, trying to get away and closer at the same time.

"So good," she bit out.

"Your tits are perfect," Wesson said then sucked as much of her breast into his mouth as he could.

Cole tugged on her nipple with his teeth before licking at the tip of as if to soothe the tiny sting. She felt that nip in her clit, her pussy gushing more of her juices because of it.

"I'm going to eat you alive," Cole told her before kissing his way down her body.

He stopped at her belly button, where he dipped the tip of his tongue inside to swirl around before he continued to her hip. He licked at the ticklish spot where her hip met her belly and tortured her before he chuckled and settled between her legs. He spread them with his shoulders so that he could lie between them.

Jessie moaned with the first touch of his mouth against the inside of her thighs. They were going to kill her. She just knew it. She would never be the same after this. For one brief instant, she wondered if she'd survive after they made love to her. Would she be forever changed? Would one man never be enough for her again?

Chapter Six

Cole spread Jessie's legs wide so that he could look at her glistening pussy and reach all of her. She was soaked for them, her juicy folds pink and waiting on his mouth. He couldn't wait to taste her but wanted her to be wild for it before he made love to her with his mouth.

He licked and kissed the insides of her thighs and all around the trimmed opening before finally licking from her slit all the way up to her clit. He blew over it then circled the little nub with the tip of his tongue. He was rewarded with her wild moan and the thrust of her hips toward him. He smiled.

"You've got the prettiest little pussy I've ever seen, Jessie."

"Please, Cole," she moaned out.

"Please, touch your pussy? Fuck it with my tongue?" he asked, breathing over her narrow opening.

"Oh, God, yes. All of it," she cried out.

He chuckled, loving that she was wild for them. He could see Wesson sucking on one tit while squeezing the other. The sight was hot and sexy to him to know his brother was taking care of her above while he was going to take care of her below. He knew she was this wild because they were both loving on her at the same time.

Cole lapped at her slit, loving the taste of her, lingering over her clit. She undulated as he lightly touched it with just the tip of his tongue. He used one hand to hold her abdomen down so he could tease and tantalize her until she was so wild with need that one touch would have her going up in flames. He wanted her wild for them, crazy with need.

He slid one finger inside her hot, wet cunt, probing until he found the sensitive spot inside of her and stroked it as he sucked on her pussy lips before circling her clit once more. When he lapped over it, she cried out, and he could feel the muscles inside of her squeezing down on the single finger he had buried knuckle deep within her.

"Please, please, please," she cried out.

"Easy, honey. I'll take good care of you," Cole told her.

She hissed out a breath as he licked lightly over her clit with just enough pressure to build her arousal without sending her over the edge. Not yet. He sucked on her pussy lips then added a second finger inside of her, thrusting the digits in and out so that she was soon rising to take in as much of him as she could.

"You're hot for us, aren't you, Jessie? You want us buried deep inside of your hot, wet cunt," Cole said.

"Yes, God, yes," she said with a low groan.

"First, I want you to come for me, darling. I want to lick all that cum from your pussy when you do. Can you come for me?" he asked.

"Yes, I'm so close, Cole. Please let me come."

He smiled then lapped at her slit while he pumped in and out of her. He licked up to her clit and licked over it several times until he felt her flutter around his fingers buried inside of her. It was then that he sucked her clit between his teeth and flicked his tongue faster over the little nub. She exploded beneath him. Her hips bucked, her voice a high keening sound as he sucked and nipped at her clit until she slowly rode the wave of her climax with him gently letting her down. The sight of her losing control between him and his brother was nothing short of amazing and had his dick so hard it ached.

He needed inside of her. He wanted to bury his cock deep in her cunt and find the pleasure they'd just given her.

"I'm going to fuck you, Jessie," he said. "I'm going to make you come all over again. Would you like that, honey?"

"I want you inside of me. I want to feel you stretch me with your hard cock, Cole."

He loved hearing her say that. Loved that she didn't shy away from wanting him.

Cole grabbed a condom out of the bedside table and rolled it on before positioning his cock at her entrance and wetting the tip with her pussy juices. He leaned over her and spread her legs with his hands before surging forward, deep inside of her. The feeling was so good he swore.

* * * *

Jessie gasped when Cole entered her. He was so big, thick, and hard inside her body. She felt filled to overflowing as he pushed inside of her in long, slow thrusts. She was still coming down from the amazing orgasm the two men had given her and could already feel the wave of pleasure building again. How was it possible that she could come a second time?

Cole stroked her in slow, frustrating penetrations until she wanted to scream at him to move faster, harder. She needed more as the pressure built inside of her. Still, he moved in slow, measured thrusts that were going to drive her insane.

Wesson distracted her with his mouth on her neck and shoulder while his fingers pulled and tugged on her nipples. The dual attention was mind-blowing, guaranteed to drive her insane with need. How could she ever go back to being with just one man after this? They were ruining her. Making her need both of them after only one night of loving.

Cole gripped her ass cheeks as he pumped his hard shaft inside her dripping cunt. She tried to lift her hips to meet him, but he controlled her movements as if needing her to be still while he fucked her.

"You're so damn wet and tight, Jessie. I'm going to come before I'm ready. You're fucking milking me, woman," Cole rasped out.

She squeezed her vaginal muscles in an effort to drive him wild so he'd give her more, give her what she wanted, what she needed. He groaned and the rhythm of his thrusts grew wilder. Then, just when she was sure she'd explode, he stopped and pulled out.

"What are you doing?" she nearly screamed out.

"Turning you over so you can suck on Wesson. He's waited patiently while we've been enjoying ourselves. Suck his cock, Jessie. Make him come with that hot little mouth of yours," Cole said.

She was suddenly on her hands and knees as Cole entered her from behind while Wesson knelt on the bed next to her head so she was able to reach his hard shaft. Jessie opened and let him guide his swollen prick between her lips. She ran her tongue along the underside then around the crown to lap at the slit, where a drop of pre-cum pearled for her taste. He tasted salty and slightly bitter, but she loved the taste of him.

Jessie sucked him down her throat, swallowing around him before letting up and returning to just the crown. His hissed-out curse told her she'd gotten to him. She licked and sucked him hard then soft. When she cupped his balls, he thread his hands through her hair and tugged lightly so that her scalp tingled along with the rest of her body. He didn't hold her still while he fucked her mouth. Instead, he allowed her to lead so that she was in control of how deep she went.

"God, you look beautiful sucking my dick, babe. I love how red and swollen your lips are around me," Wesson told her.

She groaned around him, which only had him moaning, as well. She sucked him deep then growled around him while she tugged lightly on his balls. When she scraped her nails over the heavy sac, he bit out a curse and dug his nails into her scalp. The little stings of pleasure had her working to drive him insane around her. She wanted his cum down her throat, wanted to know that she could do this to him, wanted to feel the control she welded with his pleasure.

"You're making him crazy with that wicked little mouth of yours, Jessie. Make him come so I can fuck you hard, honey. Make him shoot his load down your throat," Cole said.

He squeezed her ass cheeks as he pumped shallow, controlled thrusts inside of her as if to keep from choking her on his brother's cock.

When he circled her back hole with one finger, she moaned. She knew that if she continued seeing them that, one day, they'd want to take her back there, but she wasn't ready for that yet. Cole played with the little rosette, dipping his finger into her juices and sliding them back to the little hole. The feel of his finger there was naughty but felt good at the same time.

When he dipped one finger inside just the barest amount, she swore her pussy gushed even more around his hard cock. He pushed the finger in a little farther but didn't give her his entire finger. The pressure that built as he did that threatened to erupt over her, but she forced her concentration back on Wesson. She wanted to make him come so that Cole could fuck her until she came. She knew he was holding back, and Jessie didn't want him to hold back.

She allowed her teeth to lightly graze over Wesson's cock as she rolled his balls in one hand. He grasped her head now with both hands. She looked up at him, and his gaze was on where her mouth took his dick inside her. She twirled her tongue around the hard length of him then sucked hard on just the head. He hissed out a low curse.

Jessie pumped his cock with one hand as she increased the pace of moving up and down the hard length of him, going deep and swallowing around him until he was going wild. She dug the nails of one hand into his ass cheek while she pumped him in and out of her mouth.

Suddenly he stiffened. "I'm going to come, babe. If you don't want me to come in your mouth, you're going to have to pull back. I'm right there, babe. Right fucking there."

Jessie only sucked harder and relished the moment he erupted inside her mouth. Long, thick ribbons of his cum filled her mouth and her throat as she swallowed around him, taking all of him as he came.

"Fuck!" he shouted out. "So fucking good."

When he was spent, he pulled back from her mouth and collapsed next to her, kissing her forehead and panting as he propped himself against the headboard.

"That was amazing, babe. No one's ever made me come like that before," Wesson said.

"Hold on, babe. I'm fucking close, and this slow, easy pace is just driving me crazy," Cole told her.

She looked over her shoulder at him just before he thrust hard and deep, making good on his promise to pick up the pace. Jessie groaned at the heated feel of him deep inside of her. He thrust in then pulled out before plunging in balls deep again and again.

"I'm close, babe. So damn close," Cole ground out through gritted teeth.

Jessie cried out at the fact that she was close, too, but she still needed more, or she wouldn't make it. She shouldn't be so greedy. She'd already come once, but being this close had her antsy with need.

To her surprise, Cole seemed to know she wasn't there yet. He reached around and plucked on her clit, sending her careening over the edge with a loud cry as he pumped inside of her before losing the rhythm and following her over. The feel of him leaning over her back as he pulsed inside her felt comforting as if he sheltered her from all harm.

As she came down from the euphoria of the second orgasm, Jessie collapsed onto her elbows then her face, turning it at the last second so she could breathe. This had been amazing and scary at the same time. She knew she was going to want them both more than once. They'd wormed their way into her heart between the way they treated her and the sex. It was all so good and so dangerous at the same time.

How could she care about two men at one time? Sure, it was supposed to be a temporary fling, but this felt like more than just a one-off thing. They were courting her. She could see that now. They'd taken her on a picnic and cooked for her in their home. Was she comfortable with dating them more than once? Could she pursue a relationship with them like she was almost certain they planned on?

Suddenly her job seemed not as important as her heart. If the parents of the kids she taught didn't care that she was seeing two men at one time, then how did her heart feel about it?

Jessie jerked out of her thoughts when Cole began wiping her down with a warm wet cloth, cleaning her so that she wouldn't be sticky from her juices. Then he tossed the soiled cloth toward the bathroom and climbed up next to her on the bed on the opposite side of where Wesson was already laid out. He pulled the sheets over them and pulled her back into his arms while Wesson rolled over to fit himself at her back.

Jessie realized they planned on her staying the night. She wasn't sure how she felt about that. This was only the second date. But then she'd made love with them on the second date, so what did it matter? Besides, she was exhausted. They'd worn her out. Maybe sleeping with them wasn't so bad after all.

Chapter Seven

Jessie groaned as she rolled over to find herself alone in the bed. They had woken her up sometime around midnight and repeated the loving they'd given her the night before. She was deliciously sore and ravenously hungry. Her stomach growled at the scent of bacon frying in the kitchen.

She rolled off the bed and padded into the bathroom and took a quick shower before pulling on her clothes and following her nose. She found Cole at the stove while Wesson set the table.

"Thought the smell of food would wake you up," Cole said with a smile. "Hungry?"

"After last night I think I could eat a pig," she said with a grin.

"Figured we'd have bacon and pancakes. How does that sound?" Cole asked.

"Great. I'm definitely hungry." Jessie walked over to where Wesson was pouring juice in the glasses.

"Want some coffee?" he asked her.

"No thanks. I don't drink coffee. The juice will be fine," she said.

"If you don't drink coffee, what do you drink besides juice and water?" Wesson asked.

"Actually, I drink mostly water, but I like an occasional Diet Coke. The water is better for me, though."

"Can't do without my coffee in the morning," Wesson said. "Not sure I could function without it."

She chuckled. "Most people drink coffee as soon as they get out of bed. I just never developed the taste for it."

"First set of pancakes is ready," Cole told them.

"Let's get you set up to eat, babe," Wesson said.

Jessie watched as he set her plate on the table and moved the syrup and butter next to her. She fixed the pancakes like she liked them and dug in, marveling at the warm gooey taste of them. The bacon was just like she liked it, crisp but not burned.

"This is delicious, Cole. You can definitely cook. Dinner last night was good, too," she said.

"Hey, I may not be a good cook, but I can wash dishes like a champ," Wesson said, his mouth pulling down in a pouty frown.

"And a man who washes dishes is a rarity. Ask any woman what qualities she wants in a man and housekeeping is right up there on the list," she teased.

They ate breakfast together, talking about her job and their ranch. She enjoyed the easy conversation between them but knew she needed to get home to prepare for school the next day. Plus, she had laundry to finish up. But, Jessie didn't want to leave the comfortable bubble she'd allowed herself to exist in while there at their house, in their arms.

"Want to watch a movie?" Cole suggested once the breakfast dishes were washed and put away.

"Um, I'd really like to, but I need to get home and finish up some things before I have school tomorrow. Maybe another time?" she said.

"Hate to see you go," Wesson said, pulling her into his arms. "Are you sure you can't stay for one movie?"

"I hate to go. I really enjoyed the weekend, guys." Jessie meant every word. She had enjoyed it.

"We understand. We'll walk you to your car," Cole said.

"How about going out to the bar next weekend?" Wesson asked. "You could ask your friends to go with us."

"That sounds like fun. Saturday night?" she asked.

"Perfect. We'll call you later in the week to firm up the plans," Cole said.

They held her hands as they walked outside to where she'd parked her car. Both men pulled her into a hug and kissed her, making her want them all over again. Then they stood and watched her back out of the drive before pulling onto the road and driving off. She could still see them in her rearview mirror until she turned a curve in the road.

A shiver flowed over her at the way they made her feel. Loved, cared for, and desired. Jessie was afraid she was already becoming attached to them, and it had been only a few weeks. How would she feel after another few weeks of seeing them? What would she do if they broke things off? It would surely devastate her. She couldn't believe she'd already had sex with them. What was she thinking?

She wasn't thinking, only feeling, and they'd felt amazing to her. Where would the relationship lead them? Where did she want it to lead them? How was anything permanent even possible? Yeah, she'd talked with Angela about her relationship with her guys. They were married, and she was pregnant with their child, but could Jessie be a part of a marriage with both men?

I'm jumping ahead of myself. This might not even last that long. I need to just enjoy it while it lasts and let the future take care of itself. I can worry about it if it comes to that.

But Jessie couldn't help wondering what the future might hold.

Once she arrived home, she changed clothes and finished up the chores and double checked that she had everything ready for school the next day. She'd really had time for a movie before leaving the guys' home, but she'd felt a little too vulnerable after having spent so much time with them and the intimacy they were already building between them. She needed the space to let it settle inside of her.

The sound of her cell phone ringing in the other room jerked her out of her thoughts. Jessie picked it up on the fourth ring to find it was Brenda.

"Hey, girl. How was your date last night?" the other woman asked.

"It was good. Cole is an excellent cook," she told her.

"So you had a good time?"

"Yeah. A really good time."

"Did you stay with them overnight?" Brenda asked in a teasing voice.

"Well, um, yeah. I did," Jessie admitted. She couldn't keep anything from her friend.

"Damn, girl. Tell me all about it."

"I'm not sure what to say," she said.

"Was the sex as good as I've been told?" Brenda asked.

"Better. They're generous lovers."

"Hell, I should have hooked up with a couple before I met Tommy."

"No, you and Tommy are perfect together, and I'm not sure you would have been satisfied with him after you'd been with two men. I swear they've ruined me for one man now," she admitted.

"You're kidding. That good, huh?"

"Yeah."

"So, when are you seeing them again?" Brenda asked her.

"They want to go out to the bar next weekend. They suggested that maybe you and Tommy could come, too. What do you think?" Jessie asked.

"That sounds like fun. We can talk about it Friday night after work. Tommy and his friends are playing poker," Brenda said.

"Great. I'll be ready for pizza after my first week of school. I may only have the kids for one day, but the first week is always the hardest for me. Even when I student taught it was rough getting into the swing of things," Jessie admitted.

"Then it's a date. I'll tell Tommy about Saturday night and be sure he doesn't have something else planned."

"Great. Talk to you later." Jessie hung up and smiled.

She liked that the guys were including her friends. It was yet another reason she liked them. They were thoughtful. Really, they were too good to be true. She hoped she wasn't setting herself up for disappointment in the future.

And the future was something she was worried about all on its own.

* * * *

Wesson wiped the sweat from his forehead with the back of his arm and shook his head. They had two guys out sick, so he and Cole were working harder than normal trying to take the place of the two men out. They could both handle any part of ranching that was necessary but normally only helped here and there and directed the rest of the time. Helping to run fences or muck stalls was hard work. He appreciated all that hard work from his hands and made sure they told them that from time to time.

"My shoulders are going to give me hell tonight," Cole said as he finished up repairing the barbed wire missing from a line of fencing.

"Tell me about it. We need to work more than we do so filling in doesn't kill us," Wesson said.

"Hell, I've forgotten how to work like this."

"Me, too."

Cole dropped the fence puller into the back of the truck and grabbed a cup to get water from the cooler they'd brought with them. "Want a drink?" he asked.

"Yeah, thanks." Wesson held out his hand and grabbed the cup from Cole.

"So where should we take Jessie Saturday night to eat?" Cole asked.

"I was thinking the fish and steak house. We need to call her tonight and firm up plans. That sound okay with you?" Wesson asked.

"Suits me."

"I miss her," Cole said.

Wesson did, too. He'd had a hard time falling asleep each night and ended up jerking off to thoughts of her before he could settle down to sleep.

"Yeah. I already feel more for her than I would have thought."

"I care about her more than I would have thought, too," Cole told him.

"How do you think she feels about us?"

"I hope she cares about us more than just someone she's going out with. I hope she wants to spend more time with us."

Wesson sighed. He wanted that, as well. Hell, he had a feeling he was falling in love with her. She was sweet, intelligent, and sexy as hell. She had curves that made his mouth water and the prettiest green eyes he'd ever seen.

"Better get back to work. We've got another mile of fence to check," Cole said.

Wesson moaned. He really was going to need that hot shower when they got home. He was going to ache all over for the next few days from the hard work. Maybe they needed to pay their guys more than they were paying them. He thought about it and shook his head. Nah, they were paid pretty damn well already.

Thoughts of Jessie filled his head as they finished up work for the day. He couldn't stop thinking about her. She already consumed him with her curly brown hair and the way she smiled as if she held some secret only she knew about. Little things like the way she smiled when they talked to her and how she licked her bottom lip when she was lost in the pleasure they were giving her made his balls hurt and his heart beat harder.

Once they'd showered and dressed later that night, Cole called Jessie and put her on speaker phone so both of them could listen and talk to her.

"Hey, babe," Wesson said when she answered. "How are you doing? How's school going?"

"Hey, Wesson. I'm fine. School is good. I have the kids tomorrow, so let me tell you again later," she said with a laugh. "How are you guys doing?"

"Tired but good," Wesson said. "Cole's on with me. Are you still free Saturday?"

"Yes. I'm looking forward to it. Brenda said they can come, as well," she told them.

"Great. We thought we'd take you to the fish and steak house for dinner before the bar. How does that sound to you?" Wesson asked.

"Great. I haven't eaten there since I moved back. I used to love the fish there."

"Plan on us picking you up around six then," Cole told her. "That work for you?"

"Six is great. I'll be ready for a night out at the end of the week. What about you guys?" she asked with a laugh.

"We've had a couple of guys out sick, so we've been having to fill in. Can't wait to relax with you this weekend," Wesson told her.

"Hope you're not too tired to dance," she teased.

"Dance? That's Wesson's territory. I suck at it, remember?" Cole asked.

"No you didn't. You were fine. Besides, the fast dances Brenda and I usually dance to. Tommy won't dance them with her, so we usually dance together," she told them. "Our favorite one is "It's Raining Men".

"I'll join you on some of them, but I refuse that one", he said. "That just isn't going to happen.

Jessie laughed, the sound of it pouring over him like a welcome shower on a hot summer day. He loved her laugh.

"Deal. You can sit that one out, Wesson."

They talked for another few minutes then hung up. Wesson felt great about their date coming up and about the progress of their relationship. He'd wanted to call her every night that week but knew it was too soon to bug her like that. Hell, he wanted to talk dirty to her and have nasty phone sex, but that would have to wait until they'd created a closer relationship. Yeah, they'd had sex, but the intimacy was too new for that.

Cole stretched and sighed. "I'm beat. I'm heading to bed. I sure as hell hope Matt and Ron are back tomorrow."

"Me, too. I'm headed that way myself. My body is getting too old for actual work," Wesson said with a sigh.

"We're not forty yet, man. Don't wimp out on me."

Wesson chuckled. "I'm not. I just feel forty."

Once in bed, Wesson found that he was wide awake and hard as a rock after talking with Jessie. Thoughts of her with her mouth wrapped around his dick filled him. He grabbed the bottle of lotion next to the bed and poured a small amount into his hand and greased up his cock as he pictured her spread out before him like an all-you-can-eat buffet.

With a low groan, Wesson pumped his cock with one hand and rolled his balls with the other, thinking about fucking her in slow slides of his cock. He wanted to bury his shaft as deep as he could get then pull out and plunge back in until she was chanting his name as she drew closer to her climax. He'd grind his pelvic bone into her clit to make her come as he thrust in and out of her hot, wet cunt.

He grew closer to his climax as he pulled on his cock with long, hard jerks. The faster he tugged, the closer he got to shooting his load. He imagined seeing her come apart beneath him, and it was all it took for him to empty himself into his hand and down his shaft. Wesson groaned at the intensity of the orgasm then got up and cleaned himself up. It wasn't nearly as good as the real thing, but it had taken the edge off. He would be able to sleep now without his cock throbbing between his legs.

The last thing he thought about before falling asleep was how it would feel to wake up with her every morning for the rest of their lives.

He was so screwed.

Chapter Eight

"Dammit! We've got a cow down in the north pasture," Cole snapped. "Guys say she's breathing but unconscious."

Wesson cursed and grabbed his hat. "I'm right behind you."

Cole raced outside and saddled his horse with his brother hot on his heels. They galloped out to the north pasture where two of the hands were standing next to one of their cows scratching their heads.

When they dismounted, one of the men held up two darts. "Pulled these out of her hip."

"Fuck. I knew they were going to start experimenting before long," Cole ground out. "Wesson, call the sheriff and the vet. We need to find out if this is poison or a sedative of some kind. These kids, if they are kids, need to be stopped and soon."

He watched as Wesson walked a little ways from the group to hear as he made those phone calls. Cole wanted to hit something. They couldn't afford to have downed cows, and they sure as hell couldn't afford the possibility that it could be a person next time.

"Sheriff's on his way, and the vet should be here in about an hour. He's on the other side of town at Randy and Travis's ranch," Wesson said.

"She doesn't seem to be in any discomfort. It's probably a sedative, but where would someone get their hands on that?" Cole asked.

"Hell, where did they get a dart gun in the first place? They don't sell them in town," Wesson pointed out.

"You can get any fucking thing you want online nowadays. I'm sure they ordered it. Hell, they might have ordered the damn sedative there, as well," Cole said, running his hand through his hair.

They waited for nearly thirty minutes until the sheriff arrived. The man shook his head and took the two darts from Cole. It was obvious that the man was furious.

"Vet on the way?" he asked.

"Yeah. Be another thirty minutes before he can get here. Have you had any progress on finding out who's behind this?" Wesson asked.

"No, and it's pissing me off. I've checked with all the nearby towns, and no one is having the trouble we are, and there haven't been in sales of dart guns in the area either. Probably got it off *eBay* or some online store," the sheriff said.

"That's what we figure, as well," Cole told him.

Cole looked down at the cow and sighed. They weren't any closer to stopping whoever was behind the darts than they'd been the first time they'd found one in their horse. He worried that next time it might be one of his men or Wesson.

"I'll have the darts tested to see what exactly they used, and maybe that will help us figure out where they got it," the sheriff told them.

Just as the sheriff was pulling out, the vet pulled up and climbed out of his truck carrying a bag. His frowning face told him that he hadn't seen anything like this yet.

"So you pulled a couple of darts out of her?" he asked.

"Yeah, the sheriff is going to have them tested to see what kind of sedative they used," Cole told him.

"Probably Ketamine. If she's just sedated, she should be fine and wake up soon. Any idea how long she's been down?" he asked.

One of the hands spoke up. "We found her nearly two hours ago. She's just started twitching, so I think she's going to wake up soon."

The vet kneeled next to the cow and checked her over while Cole and Wesson watched. Sure enough the cow began moving her legs and lifting her head after another fifteen minutes.

"I can't see that she's been harmed by the drug. Once she's up on her feet again, she'll be fine. Heart sounds good, as well as her lungs. She just needs to walk the effects of the drug off is all now," the vet told them.

"So how much of a dose would it take to knock a cow this size out for at least three or four hours?" Cole asked him.

"Depends on how many darts were used and the strength of the drug. I can't really say off hand. Maybe once the sheriff gets word back on exactly what was used and the strength we can figure out the dose per dart."

"She's trying to get to her feet now," one of the hands spoke up.

They watched as the cow struggled to stand. Once she was back on her feet, Cole counted two more darts buried in the opposite side of her and pulled them out, handing them to the vet.

"That makes four darts in her to knock her out. If they did it last night, she was out a good five to six hours," Cole said.

"Whoever it is," Wesson began, "they're going to start trying it on people next. Things like this always escalate over time. They've already gone from using un-drugged darts to darts dipped in sedatives. They're going to hurt or kill someone, whether they mean to or not."

"I agree," the vet said. "Need to put a stop to this and soon. I've been to three ranches over the last few weeks, and all of them have had instances of finding darts on their cows or horses. This is the first one that they've sedated though. I guess I'll get more calls now."

Cole threaded his hands through his hair, frustration eating at his gut. He didn't want something to happen to one of his hands. Since they mostly worked during the day, and the attacks seemed to happen at night, he hoped they would be safe.

"Looks like she's doing fine now. I need to head over to the Baily ranch to vaccinate some horses. If you have anything else come up, call me," the vet said.

"Will do. Thanks for coming out," Wesson told him.

Cole followed Wesson back to the house where they tended to their horses and talked about the darts and what it could mean if one was aimed at a human.

"If they aren't using too much of the sedative, whatever it is, they might only put them to sleep, but if they don't know what they are doing, they could kill someone," Cole pointed out.

"All we can do is be on the watch and hope the sheriff can track them down soon before that happens."

"Doesn't make me worry any less."

"Me either."

They climbed the steps to the back porch and walked into the kitchen to wash up and fix sandwiches for lunch. Cole planned to work on the books for a few hours while Wesson made some calls about getting parts for the generator.

As he started on the books, thoughts of Jessie crept into his head, making him smile. He couldn't wait to pick her up later that night to go eat then out to the bar. Everything about her made him smile, from her warm brown hair to the way she moved when she walked. He could watch her ass swish back and forth all night long. Seeing her suck his brother's cock had been erotic as hell. He wanted that hot, wet mouth around his dick next time.

"I'm going to run up and shower," Wesson said, poking his head into the office.

"I'll take mine after yours. I want to finish up what I'm doing," Cole told him.

"Got those parts ordered. Should be in by Wednesday. We can pick them up after lunchtime," he said.

Cole nodded and thought that maybe they could meet Jessie for dinner that night if they waited until four to pick them up. She would be finished at school, and they could eat at the diner. That thought made him smile. He realized he was grasping at every opportunity to spend more time with her, and that was just fine with him.

* * * *

Jessie checked her reflection in the mirror one more time. She had decided on faded jeans and a long-sleeved blouse of yellow and orange to go with it. She knew it would be chilly late at night and wanted to be comfortable. She'd take a light sweater along in case she needed it.

Excitement burned through her veins at the thought of seeing the two men again. She'd thought of nothing else all week as she prepared for the students then met them on their first day. She couldn't wait to actually start teaching them literature and how it applied to present-day situations. She loved teaching about the classics and hoped to be able to interest the kids enough that they enjoyed reading them as much as she had at that age.

She wasn't naive enough to think that all of them would fall in love with them but hoped that at least a few would appreciate them and prove that by excelling in their schoolwork. She knew the hardest ones to interest would be the guys since most of them hated reading in the first place, but maybe, she could draw them in with how the classics mirrored the world today.

Jessie applied lip gloss then picked up her little purse and dropped the gloss inside before walking back to the living room to wait for the guys to arrive. Tingles of excitement burst through her bloodstream at seeing the guys again. Her pussy was already damp at the thought of feeling their arms surrounding her.

What was going on with her? She'd hadn't even known them a month yet, and already she was obsessing over them. She'd thought of little else outside of her job over the last week. Why did they attract her more than any other man she'd ever dated before?

Because they're different. I've never had two men so intent on what I needed or wanted before. I'm going to lose my heart to them if I'm not careful.

It might already be too late though. She liked them. Really liked them. They were smart, funny, and fun to be with. They'd taken her on a picnic of all things. How romantic was that?

The doorbell rang, jerking her from her thoughts. She smoothed down her blouse then ran a nervous hand through her hair before walking over to open the door. She couldn't stop the broad smile from taking over her face at the sight of the two men standing at her door.

"You look amazing," Wesson told her. His eyes twinkled as he looked her up and down.

"Beautiful," Cole added.

She felt heat blossom over her face at their flattery. "Thanks, guys."

"Ready to go?" Cole asked.

"Let me get my sweater. It's going to be cold tonight." Jessie stepped back and grabbed it off the back of the chair then locked up and allowed the two men to lead her to their truck.

"We cleaned up the work truck so we could all three sit up front. The newer truck has a console so one of us would have had to sit in the back," Wesson explained as he helped her climb into the front seat.

"I'm not picky about vehicles, guys. My Nissan is over five years old now. I don't plan on replacing it anytime soon either," she said.

"We missed you," Cole said as he backed the truck from her drive.

"I missed you guys, too," she admitted.

Thank goodness they couldn't tell her panties were already damp. Maybe she should have changed them before she left. Jessie sighed. It wouldn't have made any difference. They'd be just as wet by the time they made it to dinner anyway. They smelled delicious, like saddle oil, leather, and something citrusy. Already they were going to her head.

"How was school yesterday?" Cole asked.

"Fun but long. I forgot how exhausting it is to deal with teenagers. You'd think it would stick with me over the summer, but it must be like childbirth. Once you get past the first few days you forget all about the pain."

"Haven't heard that before," Wesson said with a chuckle.

"What made you want to be a teacher?" Cole asked.

"I used to pretend to be a teacher when I was a kid and have school with all my stuffed animals. I just always wanted to teach.

Don't know why. I like giving kids a chance to learn about the world around them before they have to jump out into it and work and live in it." Jessie shrugged. "It's not all fun, but there are moments when I see a spark in some kid's eye that makes it all worth it."

"Since you teach literature, I assume you love to read," Wesson said.

"Love, love, love it," she admitted.

"So do you only read books like Shakespeare, or do you read current books?" Cole asked.

"I read just about everything. Right now I'm reading some raunchy romance books," she told them with a wink. "Lots of romance and sex."

"You read naughty books?" Wesson asked with a wide grin.

"Yep. I just finished re-reading all of Mark Twain's books and stories and decided to read something different," she said.

I can't let them know I wanted to read more about ménage since I'm dating them.

"Wesson reads a lot of the Tom Clancy books. Have you read any of them?" Cole asked.

"Yeah. I've read most of his books. I love them. They're full of real military history, and the suspense in them is palpable. Do you read any of James Patterson's books or John Grisham?" she asked Wesson.

"I've read a couple of Grisham's books, but that's all. I don't get a lot of time to read, and I'd much rather watch a game on TV than read," Wesson admitted.

She laughed. "I bet you would. Still, it's great that you do read some."

Cole turned the truck into the parking lot of the local fish and steak house. She couldn't wait. It had been a long time since she'd eaten there. She was sure nothing much had changed. They served good food with a relaxed family atmosphere.

"Ready?" Wesson asked as he helped her down from the truck.

She nodded her head and walked between the two men. Wesson opened the door for her then followed behind Cole, who positioned himself next to her once they were inside.

"Hey, guys. Party of three?" June asked as she picked up the menus.

"That's right," Cole told her.

"Follow me," she said.

They followed behind the older woman and were seated at a table near the back of the room. Wesson held her chair for her, and then they opened their menus to decide what they wanted.

"Nothing much has changed since the last time I was here, even though the menus are new," she said.

"The food is great. Place has been in their family a long time from what I understand," Cole said.

They made their choices and gave the waitress their order before turning the conversation toward the ranch and what the two of them had been doing over the last week. She could tell something was weighing on them when they talked about work out at their place, but they didn't seem to want to talk about it. She figured it wasn't her business but couldn't help but be curious nonetheless.

They joked and laughed as they finished up, and Jessie realized that Wesson had a sense of humor more so than Cole. Where Cole was more serious and not quite as talkative as Wesson, his brother loved to talk and often joked about things even at his own expense. Jessie liked both of them just the way they were and was glad they were so different. It made dating them both not so strange.

"Ready to go?" Cole asked after a few minutes.

"I'm ready. I couldn't eat another bite. It was really good, guys."

Wesson stood and held her chair as she scooted it back and got up. She let him lead her toward the front as Cole took care of the bill. When they stepped outside to wait on the other man, Wesson pulled her close to him and brushed a kiss across her lips.

"I've been wanting to do that since we first picked you up," he said.

"You have?"

"Yeah. Your lips look delicious, and now I know they are."

"It's probably the strawberry pie I had," she teased.

"Nah, it's all you," he said.

Cole walked out and took one of Jessie's hands as they walked back to the truck. This time Cole helped her up while Wesson walked around to the driver's side and climbed in. The drive to the bar took only about five minutes. The place looked packed, but Wesson managed to find a parking place about fifty yards from the door.

Before they even stepped inside, the loud music seeped outside into the cooling night air. Jessie hoped that Brenda and Tommy were already there and had saved a table for them. Otherwise, they'd be standing around all night.

As they walked inside, she smiled at the music the band was playing. They were pretty damn good. She couldn't wait to dance with the guys. Jessie had always loved to dance, and it was one reason she and Brenda were still good friends. They both loved to dance and didn't mind dancing together when there wasn't a trusty man around.

"I see your friends over in the back. Looks like they managed to snag a table," Cole said, pointing in the general direction toward the back.

Jessie held both men's hands with her in the middle as they threaded their way through the throng of people packed shoulder to shoulder in the bar's large room. She held on tight in hopes she wouldn't get separated from them. Several times she was sure she'd lose her grip, but each time they held tight. Her fingers were going to be sore the next day after this.

"There you guys are. We were worried you wouldn't find a parking place and give up," Brenda said, jumping up to hug Jessie.

"Managed to find one not too far away," Cole told them.

"Tommy, Brenda, you've met Cole, and this is his brother, Wesson Taylor," Jessie said by way of introductions.

"How are you doing, Tommy?" Wesson asked, holding out his hand.

"Fine. It's good to meet you," Tommy said, shaking Wesson's then Cole's hand.

They all talked about the band and ordered drinks. Then Brenda jumped up and grabbed Jessie's hand when a fast song started up.

"We'll be back in a little bit," she told the men. "This is one of our songs."

Jessie laughed and allowed her friend to pull her to the dance floor. At least she wouldn't have to talk about how things were going with her and the guys while they were dancing. There was no way anyone could hold a conversation in front of the band. They were just too loud.

After two fast numbers, they slowed things down, and she and Brenda made their way back to the men. They appeared to be in deep conversation when they walked up but broke apart as they took their seats. Jessie wondered what they'd been talking about since all three men looked serious as hell when they'd approached the table. Their faces brightened immediately when they caught sight of them.

The rest of the night went great as she danced with both men and Brenda until she was sure her legs were going to fall off. She hadn't had that much exercise since taking tennis lessons in college. She was exhausted.

"Looks like they're going to be closing the place down soon. You guys ready to call it a night?" Cole asked.

"Lord, I'm toast. Take me home, Tommy," Brenda said with a sigh as she leaned her head against his shoulder.

"You're toast, and you're tanked. I sure hope you can walk on your own cause I'm too worn out to carry your ass," Tommy teased.

"I'm not drunk. Just a little tipsy," she protested then hiccupped.

They all laughed at that. Jessie couldn't help smiling. Her entire face hurt from smiling so much. She hadn't had this much fun in years. Part of it was spending time with Brenda, but a good part of it was being with Cole and Wesson. They treated her like a woman as well as a friend. She was fast becoming attached to the two of them, and that could lead to heartache if things didn't work out between the three of them.

And what if it did? Was she willing to make what they had permanent in the future? Married to two men? Jessie wasn't sure how to answer that and was only glad she didn't have to anytime soon.

Chapter Nine

The next several weeks flew by as Jessie taught all week and spent her weekends with the guys. They took her out to eat or cooked for her at their home. She was fast getting way too attached to them for her own good. She was afraid that something would change and they would go their separate ways. Jessie knew it would devastate her. She was falling for them. Falling for the way they made her feel like the most important person in the world to them and falling for their devastating good looks and sexy bodies.

She pulled on her boots just as she heard their truck pull up outside. They were going horseback riding and on another picnic. Saturday had dawned cool and clear. It wouldn't be long before October rolled around. Jessie knew that this might be the last chance at having a picnic for the year. Hopefully the warm sun would make up for the cooler temperature.

"Hey, Jessie. You look great. Be sure and grab a coat just in case it gets colder," Cole said as he stepped inside the house.

"Wesson in the truck?" she asked.

"No. He's getting the horses ready for us,"

"Must have lost the coin toss," she teased.

Cole smiled. "Yeah. One of us had to stay behind and saddle them up. Didn't want to miss one second of spending time with you."

She felt the blush heat her cheeks. "Me, too. You guys always make me feel good."

He pulled her closer and dipped his head to claim her lips with his. She melted in his arms as he slanted his mouth across hers and probed at her lips with his tongue. The instant she opened to him he was sliding his against hers and pulling all sorts of moans and groans from her as he devoured her mouth.

When he pulled back, they were both panting with veils of lust clouding their eyes. Jessie knew that if they didn't hurry up and get going, they'd end up being very late for their picnic. She cleared her throat and took a step back to grab her coat.

"We'd better go now," she said.

"Yeah. I think you're right."

She let him help her into the truck then buckled the seatbelt as Cole started the truck and backed out of her drive. They rode in silence, but Cole took her hand in one of his and held it the entire trip out to the ranch. When they pulled up outside the barn, Wesson strode across the ground and helped her down.

"Was about to call and check on you two. I was going to ask what took you so long, but I think I can guess by the color in your cheeks, babe." Wesson grinned down at her.

It still surprised her that the two men never got jealous over each other. The longer she spent with them, the more secure she felt that they weren't going to suddenly fight over her. It made her spending time with them so much easier and more relaxing since she didn't have to constantly think about who she'd last kissed or held hands with.

"Ready for a picnic?" Wesson asked.

"Can't wait. What's for lunch?" she asked.

"That's a secret," Wesson said with a wide grin nearly splitting his face in two.

"Please tell me Cole cooked and you didn't," she said with mock horror.

Wesson narrowed his eyes at her and shook his head. "You wound me."

Jessie just rolled her eyes and allowed him to help her climb on the back of the horse then waited for them to mount up, as well. They rode for well over an hour before Cole stopped them to take a walking break. Jessie rode with them fairly frequently, but she still wasn't as used to a saddle as they were. The brief walk always did her good.

"How are you feeling?" Wesson asked as she stretched her arms over her head.

"I'm good. You guys have just about put the cowgirl back into me," she said.

Cole smiled. "She was never gone. Just waiting for her time to come back out and shine."

Jessie loved how they were always paying her compliments. What woman could ever refuse them? Why hadn't they found someone before now? They were amazing men with so much going for them.

"Ready to go?" Wesson asked.

"Yeah. I'm getting hungry," she said.

They rode for another two hours before they stopped among a grove of trees where they spread out the blanket and began unpacking lunch.

"Yummy!" Jessie squealed with delight. "Homemade chicken salad. I can't wait."

Wesson laughed. And before you are allowed to eat you have to tell me how good I did."

"What do you mean?" she asked.

"I actually boiled the eggs that went into it. Ask Cole. I did it without him even in the room." He stuck his chin in the air and smiled.

"I'm proud of you, Wesson. What made you want to boil the eggs?" she asked.

"Just wanted to prove that I could do something in the kitchen besides clean up Cole's messes." Wesson grinned.

"I don't make messes," Cole said, his brows furrowed together.

Jessie and Wesson looked at each other and grinned. "Yes you do," they said together.

"Whatever. Let's eat." Cole handed bread to Jessie, and the three of them made sandwiches and ate potato chips.

After they'd finished and put everything away, they laid back on the blanket and talked about what was going on in town or the latest gossip about someone. Before she knew it, Jessie had drifted off to sleep.

* * * *

Something tickled Jessie's nose. She batted at it then finally opened her eyes to see Wesson leaning over her with a flower stem hanging above her face.

"'Bout time you woke up. You've just about slept the entire afternoon away," he said with a wide grin.

"Why didn't you wake me up sooner?" she asked, sitting up.

"Because we slept just as long as you did," Cole muttered. "Can't believe we fell asleep."

"We must have needed it, or we wouldn't have done it," Wesson said.

"Hate that we missed so much time with you, Jessie," Cole continued.

"I still had a good time, guys," she said.

Wesson leaned over and kissed her, brushing his lips lightly over hers then deepening the kiss so that Jessie moaned into his mouth. He felt amazing covering her like he was doing and rocking her world with his lips on hers. Then she felt Colt kissing down her neck and one hand squeezing her breast as Wesson continued to tease her with his tongue.

"As much as I want to continue this, I think we need to do so at the house. It's going to get colder soon, and it gets dark earlier every day now," Cole reminded them.

She sighed as Wesson moved from over her to climb to his feet. He held out his hand to help her up.

Jessie stood and stretched then helped fold the blanket before carrying some of the empty containers to where Cole was packing them on his horse.

"We'll watch a movie when we get back home," Wesson said. "Cole has stew on the stove for us to eat. He just has to make cornbread to go with it."

"That sounds great. What movie are we watching?" she asked as he helped her up on her horse.

"*Pacific Rim*," Wesson told her.

"I love that movie," she said with a smile.

They'd ridden for nearly an hour when Jessie felt something sting the back of her left shoulder. She tried to slap at it but couldn't reach it.

"Damn."

"What's wrong, hon?" Wesson asked, riding up next to her.

"Something bit me on my shoulder. I can't reach it to rub at it.

"Hey, Cole. Stop for a second.

"What's wrong?" he asked, turning to trot up next to them.

"Let me look, Jessie," Wesson said.

"Guys, I don't feel so good." Jessie's vision was blurring, and her head felt weird.

"What's wrong?" Cole asked again.

"Fuck! There's a dart in her shoulder."

Wesson's voice sounded so far away. Why was there a dart in her shoulder? They weren't playing darts. They were riding horses, right? Then everything went black.

Chapter Ten

Cole and his brother paced in the waiting room of the emergency room. He hated not knowing what was going on with Jessie. They weren't allowed in back until the doctor had seen her, and the waiting was killing him. He could see by the lines on Wesson's face that it was having the same effect on him.

They'd managed to dismount and catch Jessie before she'd fallen off the horse but had to drape her over the horse to get her home and to the waiting ambulance. He'd called them to meet them at the house the minute they had her settled on the horse then led it back to their home as fast as they could safely go with her across the saddle like they had her.

"What do you think is going on back there?" Wesson asked.

"I don't know. Where is the fucking sheriff?" Cole asked.

"He was out on a call. He'll be here as soon as he can."

"Something has to be done about this and soon," Cole said.

"I'm not so sure we're dealing with teenagers now. I can't imagine them harming a woman. Cattle? Yes, but not a woman."

"I think you're right. This is some kind of sick bastard getting his kicks out of hurting animals and, now, people."

Cole ran a hand through his hair just as the sheriff strode into the waiting room. His face was taut with rage as he joined them.

"How is she?" he immediately asked.

"We don't know anything yet. The doctor is supposed to come out and give us an update, but he hasn't yet," Cole told the other man.

"This has got to stop. Where is he getting the drugs?" Wesson asked.

"I'm researching online to find out if you can buy ketamine without a prescription, but there are quite a few places. Did you know it's used to treat depression? Hell, people even snort the stuff. You wouldn't believe the chatter on the internet about the crap," the sheriff said.

"If he can get it online, you might never find out who it is," Cole said.

"That's what has me worried. Catching this guy isn't going to be easy," the sheriff admitted.

"Well, fuck." Wesson stuck his hands on his hips and frowned.

"I'm going to go out where it happened and see if I can find anything that the man might have left while he waited for you guys. I'm sure he was watching you and picked a spot to ambush you from. He might have left something behind I can use to find him," the sheriff said.

"Until he is caught," Wesson said. "No one is safe just doing their job. The hands might be safe out in the middle of nowhere, but any of them riding fences or near any trees where the man can hide are at risk."

"Everyone needs to stay in twos so that if one of them get shot, the other can get help," the sheriff said.

"Hell, he could shoot both of them just as easily as shooting one of them," Cole pointed out.

"It's the best I can do until I figure out who he is." The sheriff shook his head. "I know it isn't much, but it's all I've got."

"If all they used was the ketamine, why was she still unconscious when they got her to the hospital?" Cole asked.

"I don't know. Maybe they increased the dose or changed to another kind of drug since they were planning to use it on people next," the sheriff said.

"We've got to stop this sick bastard before someone dies," Wesson said.

"I'm doing all I can do. We've no idea where he'll strike or when. I don't have the first clue how to identify him. I'm having a friend monitor *Facebook* and *Twitter* to see if someone boasts about what they are doing. I'm praying he'll feel the need to gloat over what he's doing and we'll see it online." The sheriff looked up just as the door leading back to the emergency room whooshed open and a man in scrubs stepped through them.

He walked over to where Cole, Wesson, and the sheriff were standing by the windows.

"Are you with Miss Winters?" he asked.

"That's right. How is she?" Wesson asked.

"She's coming around nicely. She's going to be woozy and a little confused for a few hours, but the effects are wearing off nicely. The dart had to be coated with enough of the drug to knock her out for a good three hours. That's a fairly strong dose," he told them.

"Do you know what was used?" the sheriff asked.

"She tested positive for valium. I know that you suspected it to be ketamine, but it wasn't. Valium was in her system," the doctor said.

"Can we see her?" Wesson asked.

"Yes. Just remember that she's going to be a little off for another hour or so. I want to monitor her for any side effects before I discharge her. She'll be able to go home after that." The doctor led the way to the back and the room where they were treating Jessie.

Once they walked into the room, Cole immediately felt a sense of relief. Jessie's color was much better than when they'd watched her being loaded into the ambulance earlier. She turned her head toward them when they entered the room. The woozy smile that blossomed across her face had his heart flipping in his chest.

"Hey there, beautiful," Cole said. "How are you feeling?"

"A little spacy, but fine. The doctor said I was shot with a dart. I don't remember anything except going on a picnic with you guys," she said.

"We are so sorry this happened, Jessie," Wesson said.

"It wasn't your fault guys. It was whoever shot me. Why would someone want to shoot someone like that?" she asked.

"I don't know. He must be crazy to harm another human being. It's bad enough to target animals, but he's taking it a step further to risk hurting a person. The sheriff is looking into it, but catching this guy is going to be hard. No more picnics until the man is caught," Wesson said.

Cole agreed with him. They weren't about to risk Jessie getting hurt again.

He realized in that moment that he had fallen in love with her. She meant the world to him, and the idea of something happening to her had his stomach cramping and his heart racing to the point of making him dizzy.

What if it had been poison on that dart? The thought of her dying nearly brought him to his knees.

* * * *

Jessie's mouth was parched as she listened to the guys go over the last few hours with her. She still couldn't believe that she'd been shot and knew she'd been lucky. It could have been so much worse. The dart could have had poison of some kind on it. Why would someone want to hurt someone else? She knew that there were crazy people in the world, but she'd never believed that someone from her home would be capable of that.

I've forgotten that the town is growing and more people are moving here. I guess bad people are everywhere.

She hated to think that her idyllic home could possibly be home to someone so cruel and lacking in morals. What if it had been a teenager or someone even younger? Would it have hurt them even worse than it had harmed her?

Jessie could still feel the wooziness an hour later as the guys helped her off the stretcher to walk to the bathroom. She wasn't sure she could have made it without them helping her to stand and walk. Her legs felt like spaghetti noodles.

"How are you feeling?" Cole asked her for the dozenth time.

"I'm okay. The fogginess in my head is almost gone," she told him.

"That's good. The doc said it would linger for a little while. Are you sure you're ready to go home?" Wesson asked. "Maybe you should stay here for another couple of hours to be safe."

"The doctor said I could go home now. I want my own bed. This stretcher isn't all that comfortable." Jessie tried to smile at the two men, but her face felt odd.

"We'll get you home and make sure you're comfortable. We aren't leaving you tonight. I won't be able to sleep worrying about you," Wesson said.

Jessie liked that they wanted to take care of her. Still, she was going to be just fine. They didn't have to hover over her. It would get to be annoying after a while. She hoped they weren't going to do that. It would spoil some of how she felt for them. Right now, she was more than a little in love with them, and it scared her. They'd only known each other for a little over a month. That was too short a time to fall in love, right?

Maybe love at first sight does happen. I've just never known it to happen before.

Jessie realized that she wanted it to be true, wanted to really love them. Wanted them to really love her, as well. When had her mind changed about being with two men? She wasn't even all that worried about her job now. Of course she doubted many people at school even knew she was dating Wesson and Cole. Yet so far nothing had come of her worry that they'd fire her on moral grounds. The town really did seem to be mostly accepting of the threesome couples that lived there.

I want this to work out. I want the two men in my life for more than boyfriends. I want it all.

And she did. Jessie smiled, unable to keep the thoughts inside any longer. She loved Cole and Wesson, but she wanted them to say the words to her first. She didn't want to risk that they weren't in love with her, as well, before she blurted out that she loved them.

The idea that they might not feel the same way helped her keep from blurting out the words when they focused their attention on her while she redressed. It took both men to help her into her clothes because she kept losing her balance in the process.

"Ready to head home?" Cole asked.

"Yes. Thanks, guys. I really appreciate you helping me and staying with me. I wouldn't have wanted to lie here all alone with my head swimming like it was." She smiled at both men.

"There was no way in hell we were going to leave you here while you were recovering," Wesson said, frown lines appearing between his brows.

"Still, I appreciate it," she said.

"I'll pull the truck around," Cole said.

Jessie accepted the ride in the wheelchair from the nurse, and with Wesson's help, she climbed into the truck and settled in the front seat with Wesson taking the back seat behind her. They were silent all the way to her house. Each man seemed to be deep in thought, and hers were so muddled form the remnants of the drug that she had a difficult time just keeping her eyes open.

Once she was settled on the couch at her place, the men settled in with her feet on Wesson's lap and her head on Cole's as they watched TV and she dozed. It felt comfortable lying there between them. It felt right. With that thought in her head, she drifted lazily between consciousness and sleep until the game they'd been watching was over.

"Are you hungry?" Cole asked her.

Jessie roused enough to think about it. She was a little hungry.

"I should probably eat something. I'm a little hungry but don't think I want anything heavy," she said.

"How about eggs and toast?" Cole asked.

"Yeah. That sounds good."

Cole left her with Wesson and retreated to the kitchen to whip up the meal. Wesson massaged her feet with what she thought was a worried expression tightening his face.

"I'm okay, Wesson," she finally said.

"I know, but you might not have been. It kills me that it happened while we were just out riding on our land. The bastard is trespassing, and we didn't even know he was there."

"It's not your fault. I don't blame either of you guys."

"I know. Doesn't mean I am any less upset over it, though."

"I understand, Wesson. Just don't let it make you sick thinking about it. It's over, and I'm just fine." She poked him in the chest with her toe.

He grunted then smiled. It transformed his rugged good looks from the frowning angry look to one of contentment as he squeezed her foot.

They ate in silence then Cole had insisted that they head to bed. He wanted her to sleep off the remainder of the effects of the drug, and they were going to stay the night to be sure she didn't need anything during the night. Jessie was just fine with that idea. Having them close to her always felt good.

It felt right and normal to her now. She loved having them surrounding her in the bed. She felt safe and happy between them. She just hoped they would grow to love her as much as she did them.

The men undressed her as if she were a china doll, taking extra care to be sure she didn't get off balance. They tucked her in with a kiss then undressed, as well, to slip into the bed on either side of her. She curled around Wesson with Cole plastered to her back. She wanted to enjoy the feel of them pressed so close to her body, but the effects of the drug still lingered, and she fell asleep almost immediately to thoughts of the three of them falling in love. It made her smile.

Chapter Eleven

Jessie still felt a little off the next day but counted herself lucky that there hadn't been anything more dangerous on the dart that had knocked her out. She'd also been lucky that she hadn't fallen off the horse and broken her neck before the guys had grabbed her.

Wesson and Cole spent the day with her, catering to her and spoiling her with their insistence of doing everything for her. They even hovered near the bathroom door when she had to go. It was both sweet and cloying at the same time. She just hoped that it would all settle down by the next time she spent time with them. She couldn't handle being smothered by them all the time.

I honestly love how they care so much about me, but I don't like being babied. This will never work if they keep this up.

"How about watching a movie on the couch," Cole suggested.

"Sure," she said. "Want to see what's on Netflix or Hulu?"

"Good idea," Cole agreed.

They settled her on the couch with a glass of lemonade and set next to her with Cole scrolling through the possibilities. They finally settled on an action flick and relaxed as the movie started. Both men held one of her hands after she'd given up her glass of lemonade. They both seemed to want to touch her a lot since the incident with the dart. It was sweet, but she hoped they weren't constantly going to start smothering her.

One movie turned into two, along with a bowl of popcorn and a bowl of peanuts. She thoroughly enjoyed the quiet time with them. Well, quiet time wasn't exactly right since they all cheered with the hero and heroine and booed the villains together. She realized she liked that about them. It was something she'd always done, and they seemed to enjoy it, as well.

"It's getting late, babe," Wesson said. "Neither of us want to go, but you need your rest before school tomorrow and we need to get back to check on the ranch. Are you sure you're going to be okay to go to work tomorrow?"

"I'm sure. I really feel fine now. I think the effects of the drug have completely worn off," she assured him.

"If you need anything at all, day or night, call us, Jessie. We mean it," Cole said.

"I will. I'll be fine. You're right. I really need to get some rest before I have to deal with teenagers tomorrow. I'm going to gather my things for school then go on to bed early," she told them. "Thanks for everything. Helping me yesterday and staying the night with me."

"We care about you, Jessie. There was no way we were going to leave you alone after you'd been hurt. Now lock up behind us," Wesson said as he and Cole headed for the door.

Cole pulled her into his arms and kissed her, rubbing his hands up and down her back as he did. The kiss was chaste compared to their usual heated ones, but it warmed her from the inside out. He placed another kiss on her nose then turned her to Wesson.

Wesson didn't baby her with his kiss. He kissed her as if he might never see her again. His mouth ate at hers before sucking her bottom lip into his mouth and teasing it with the tip of his tongue. When he finally let her go, she was dizzy, but it had nothing to do with the drug. It had everything to do with his kiss and how she felt about the man. He undid her with how much passion he put into everything he did to her.

Where Cole was easy and relaxed around her, loving on her with playfulness and warmth, Wesson was passionate, giving his all and demanding it back from her. They were so different but complemented each other perfectly. She loved them both and knew that if they grew tired of the relationship it would devastate her.

It's too late to put a stop to it now. Losing them will kill me. I'm in too deep.

Jessie locked the door behind them after promising to get some rest and be safe. She listened as the truck started up then backed out of the drive to rumble down the road. She stayed next to the door until she could no longer hear them then hugged herself. The house was already too empty without them there with her.

She puttered around cleaning up and gathering her supplies for school the next day then took a shower and climbed into bed with her Kindle to read until she felt sleepy enough to turn off the light and go to sleep.

She couldn't concentrate on the book enough to know what she was reading. Instead, thoughts of the men and how they made her feel kept intruding on the storyline. She shivered as she remembered their touch and how her heart skipped a beat when they kissed her. She sighed and put aside the e-reader and snuggled down under the covers. Before she finally fell asleep, she realized that she could still smell them in her bed. Strangely enough that helped her relax enough to drift off.

* * * *

"I didn't want to leave her there alone," Cole said as they drove toward home.

"Neither did I, but we can't run a ranch from there," Wesson said.

"I love her, man. I want her to move in with us."

"Yeah, me, too. She's perfect for us."

Wesson wanted her to marry them even more than he wanted her to just move in with them. He loved her so much it scared him at times. Falling for Jessie this soon had surprised him. He'd expected it to be just like all the other women they'd dated. Either they broke it off because she couldn't handle both of them or they broke it off because the woman just wasn't who they were looking for.

He sighed. "Convincing her to move in with us this soon isn't going to happen, Cole. We've got to take this slow so we don't spook her. We talked about this."

"That was before someone shot her with the fucking dart. I want her close to us so we can watch over her," Cole said.

"As much as I agree that I want her close, she'd be in more danger living with us right now than living in town. The bastard who's doing this is concentrating on ranches where he can more easily hide. I don't want her near our place until he's caught and stopped," Wesson said.

"Fuck, I know you're right, but I miss having her in my arms at night during the week."

"Me, too."

"Hell. I can't believe I've fallen this fast for her," Cole said.

"Just proves that she's the one for us." Wesson turned down the road that led to their ranch.

"I hate that we can't bring her out to our place anymore," Cole said.

"We can still cook for her and have her over to watch movies, but no more horseback riding until the sheriff catches this asshole." Wesson slowed for the turn down their long drive.

"We need to help him stop this guy. We can hunt him as sure as he's been hunting on our ranch," Cole said.

"I was already thinking that. We should get with all the other ranchers in the area and form a plan. Once the sheriff has finished looking over where Jessie got shot, we can do our own investigation," Wesson told him.

Once he'd parked in front of the house, Wesson climbed out of the truck and looked around their yard. There weren't any trees near the house, only the outbuildings like the barn, the tool shed, and the equipment shed. Behind them was their land spreading out as far as he could see and then farther. Somewhere out there a bully, because that was ultimately what the bastard was, had been stalking first their cattle then their woman.

"What are you thinking?" Cole asked with one foot on the back steps leading up to the porch.

"That whoever this is, he's a bully. He's either been terrorizing people since childhood or was terrorized and is trying to take control by picking on other people from a safe distance where he can't get hurt anymore."

"You might be right."

"I am right. I can feel it."

"So how does that help us catch him?"

"I don't know, but we're going to catch the son of a bitch one way or another."

Wesson looked out around the yard one more time then followed his brother inside. He grabbed a beer from the fridge and tossed one to Cole. They walked into the living room and sat down without turning the TV on. Neither of them felt like watching it anyway. They were deep in their own thoughts, wondering who the man was behind the shootings.

He wondered if it would turn out to be someone they knew, someone who'd worked their ranch or someone they'd met in town. What did all the ranches hit have in common? He planned to find out tomorrow. Maybe it was as simple as someone who they'd all fired at some point and now he was trying to get back at them.

"Can you remember the names of everyone we've fired in the last three years?" Wesson asked.

"Maybe, but it would be easier to look back at the payroll books. Are you thinking that he could be someone with a grudge? What about the other ranches?"

"We compare names with them. He might have been fired from the other ranches, as well," Wesson suggested.

"Good idea. Even if we only get a couple of the other ranchers having fired the same man, it's a start. The other ranches could just be to throw everyone off," Cole said.

"That's what I'm thinking. I'll call the sheriff in the morning and see what he thinks. We'll dig through the books and make a list of those men we've fired over the last few years."

"It's hard to believe someone would be pissed enough to shoot a human. Hitting us using our animals is one thing, but targeting a human, and especially a woman is wrong on so many counts. That's just too fucked up," Cole said.

"I agree, but someone is out there hunting people now, and it's only a matter of time before he switches from darts to real bullets."

"Damn, I was hoping I was the only one who was worried about that. But you're right. It's only a matter of time."

Wesson finished his beer and set the empty bottle on the coffee table before propping his feet up on the table. He felt like they would know the man responsible once he was captured, and that bothered the shit out of him. It felt as if they would know that someone who could do something like this would stick out to him, but he honestly couldn't think of a single soul he would have believed could shoot someone, much less a woman. He prayed it turned out to be someone from another town and not someone he knew.

"I don't know what I would do if something happened to Jessie," Cole said out of the blue.

"Me either. She's ours, Cole. She's ours, and I'm not going to sit around until that bastard screws up and gets caught. I'm going to hunt for him," Wesson said.

"How?"

"I don't know yet, but I'm going to scour every inch of our land to find out where all he's been and see if I can narrow down who he is by his footprints and whatever else he might have left behind to give himself away. The sheriff can't do it all. He's only got two deputies, so he's spread too thin to spend all his time on it. He needs help, and I'm going to give it to him," Wesson said.

"Talk to the other ranchers and see if they can go over their land, as well. You can all compare what you find and see if you can come up with a likely suspect. I'll get the names of our ex-employees, and you can compare with them while I see to the ranch." Cole leaned forward, resting his elbows on his knees. "I'm with you. We've got to take matters into our own hands and help the sheriff find this guy and fast."

"I'm just glad that Jessie lives in town and is at work all day. She's safer there than she would be just about anywhere else," Wesson said.

"I agree. As much as I want her here where we can watch out for her, it's not safe right now. I'm worried about the other ranchers who have children at home. Surely the asshole won't shoot a kid," Cole said, shaking his head.

"I don't know. I never would have thought he'd shoot a woman, but he did."

"We've got to find him."

"Find him and stop him," Wesson said.

Cole stretched and stood. "I'm going to grab a shower then head to bed. It's going to be a long day tomorrow."

"I'm right behind you. I'm anxious to get started looking for clues," Wesson told his brother.

Once Cole had strode away, Wesson tried to think back to everyone they'd fired that he could remember. Most of them had been angry about being let go, but there were a couple who stood out as especially upset to the point of threatening. He couldn't remember their names, but he could see their faces in his mind. If any of those men had also been fired at the other ranches, they'd at least have a suspect pool to investigate.

Wesson sighed. They'd turn the names over to the sheriff because he had the expertise in interrogation. All he would be able to do is beat it out of them. That wouldn't go over too well with anyone involved. He didn't want to look like a brute to Jessie. He'd let the sheriff handle it, even though, deep down, he wanted to do it himself.

Finally, Wesson felt like he could shower and relax enough to go to bed. He was sure he'd still see Jessie's unconscious body on that stretcher in his sleep. It haunted him how pale she'd been and how shallow her breathing had seemed. For a while, he'd feared they'd lose her before they'd even begun to know her. It caused a deep ache beneath his breast bone.

The sound of the shower shutting off in Cole's room galvanized Wesson into getting to his feet and walking toward his room. Thoughts of how close they'd come to possibly losing Jessie haunted him all through his shower, following him to his bed. He prayed he didn't have nightmares about it once he finally fell asleep. More than that, he prayed their Jessie didn't have them while she was all alone. One of them should have stayed with her, but it was too late now.

Chapter Twelve

Jessie's week flew by amid laughter, groans, and excitement from her students. They were a great bunch of kids to work with, but there were always a few who resisted the draw of literature and complained about it nonstop. She tried to mix up what they read and discussed with some more interesting books that she had hoped would pique the interest of the worst of the class. It didn't always work.

"What about *The Odyssey* bores you?" she asked one student.

"It's just so out there. Why can't we read something from now?" he asked.

"So, how many of you have watched the movies Percy Jackson or read the books?" she asked.

Most everyone in the room raised their hands, including the two reluctant teenagers who were complaining about what they were supposed to be studying now.

"Well, those were based on *The Odyssey*," she told them.

"No way," someone said.

"Yes, just think about it. What were some of the monsters he fought in those movies?" she asked.

After that, everyone settled in to read and comment about how the movie differed from the book or how the movie got it right. The afternoon went by much quicker with her other class when she brought up the Percy Jackson movies with them, as well.

I should have thought about this a long time ago.

By the end of the day she felt better about how classes were going and wanted nothing more than to go home, prop up her feet and enjoy reading something she wanted to read for a change. Namely, one of her naughty romance novels.

"What has that smile on your face? I know it can't be about work," Laney said.

Laney was one of the other teachers, who taught science. They'd instantly bonded over the joys of teaching mini adults with attitudes the size of giants.

"Just thinking about how much I'm going to enjoy propping my feet up once I get home," she said.

"Tell me about it. These kids keep me on my feet all day just trying to keep up with them."

"Yeah. Coming up with ways to keep them interested in all this *dry* literature"—she air quoted the word dry—"has got to be the hardest thing I've ever done. They hate the classics and barely tolerate some of the other books I have them read."

"How are you feeling after your trip to the hospital Saturday?" Laney asked out of the blue.

"Wow, news travels fast. I'm fine. No ill effects at all."

"You were incredibly lucky," the other woman said.

"I know. It could have been poison or something I was allergic to," Jessie agreed.

"I sure hope they catch the person behind it and soon."

"Me, too."

Jessie told the other woman bye and gathered up her books and purse to head home. She'd only made it as far as the end of the hall when Glen Brooks, the assistant principal, stopped her.

"How are you doing today?" he asked, touching her elbow.

"I'm good. Thanks. How are you doing?" she asked with a broad smile.

"Fine, fine. I'm more concerned about you. I hope you're not going back out to that ranch after what happened," he said.

"No more horseback riding, but the guys want me to come have supper again this weekend," she told him.

"Do you really think it's a good idea to date two men, Jessie?" he asked.

"That's personal, Glen."

"Not when it affects your job it isn't."

"How will seeing Cole and Wesson affect my job? I only see them on the weekends, so it doesn't have anything to do with work." Jessie felt heat burn her cheeks.

"It's not normal, Jessie. People are beginning to talk, and that isn't good for a teacher's career," he said with a slight sneer tightening his features.

"Since it's my career, I'd appreciate it if you wouldn't lecture me about it. I can make my own decisions, Glen."

Jessie stalked off, leaving him standing in the hall behind her. Fury beat in her belly like a bat flapping its wings in an effort to get out of the daylight. She couldn't believe he'd threatened her like that. It was a threat. He was holding her future as a teacher over her head because she was seeing two men. It was what she'd originally worried about when she'd started seeing Cole and Wesson in the first place. Now, after having met so many other women who were married to two men, she didn't think he could hurt her job as a teacher, but a nagging feeling still burned deep in her gut.

I love teaching. I got my masters so that I could teach. What if my being with both men jeopardizes that?

The thoughts churning around in her head had her hands shaking as she started her car and pulled out of the parking lot to drive home. Surely they wouldn't fire her for it. There were so many other families in town who were threesomes. Their kids were in school now. She didn't teach them yet, but she would eventually. Was it enough to discourage anyone from firing her? Jessie didn't know.

By the time she'd gotten home, Jessie was all worked up and afraid for her job. She changed clothes and pulled on a pair of jeans and a T-shirt. Now she'd never be able to settle down and read. Instead, she called her best friend, Brenda.

"Hey, girl. How's school going?" the other woman asked when she'd answered her phone.

"Classes are great. You know how much I love to teach."

"There's a but in there. What's up?"

"The assistant principal stopped me in the hall and essentially threatened my job if I continued seeing Cole and Wesson. He actually said it wasn't normal and that people were talking. What if he gets me fired?"

"Oh, hon. That's not going to happen. There are too many people living here who are fine with the threesomes living here. Try not to worry about it. I'll call Gale Finnwick who's on the school board and talk to her about it. She'll talk to the others and make sure your personal life isn't going to affect your job," Brenda said.

"Do you think she can do that? The principal is the one who can fire me, and the assistant principal is his right-hand man."

"True, but if they reach out to him and tell him it wouldn't be in his best interest as an employee of the school district to do so, I think he'll think twice about it."

"I hope you're right, Brenda. I can't afford to lose my job, and now I don't want to lose the guys. I've gotten really attached to them," she told the other woman.

"Are you in love with them?" Brenda asked with what sounded like glee in her voice.

"Um, I think it's too soon to say that," she lied.

Somehow admitting it to her friend made it all the more real, and Jessie needed time to get used to the feeling herself before she said anything to Brenda. Once her friend knew about it, there would be no stopping her from trying to plan Jessie's wedding as well as her own. She had no idea how the men felt at this point. Sure she knew they cared about her. They'd more than proved that with how attentive they'd been ever since she'd started dating them. Still, she needed to hear it from their mouths before she could say the words herself. She was scared that it would all be one-sided.

They talked about work and the wedding and how excited Brenda was. She had only two more months before the big event. Jessie was happy for her friend and enjoyed helping her plan the big event.

Once they'd hung up, Jessie felt a little better and settled down in her favorite chair to try and relax and read.

Chapter Thirteen

"I've contacted all the other ranches that have been affected by this guy and compared names of men we've fired," Cole told Wesson. "Funny thing is that the only ranches affected are those where they're either in a ménage relationship or are actively looking for a woman to share."

"That's too much to be just a coincidence," Wesson said.

"I agree. There are two men we all have in common as having fired. I'm going to run into town and talk to the sheriff about them," Cole told his brother.

"Good idea. Did you find anything when you rode around the ranch?" Wesson asked.

"No. He covered his tracks well."

"He had to have left something behind. We've got a lot of territory out there. Maybe you missed something," Cole said.

"It's possible. Like you said, there's a lot of ground to cover. I'll keep looking after I talk with the sheriff. The best place will be where Jessie was shot. We don't have a clue about where the horse or the cows were originally shot."

"I've got the ranch work covered here. Concentrate on finding this guy. I don't want anything to happen when we have Jessie over this weekend for dinner. I'm still not sure it's a good idea with this bastard still out there," Cole said.

"She'll be inside with us. It should be safe," Wesson said.

"Maybe. We'll keep her away from windows, too. All of this has me spooked."

"Me, too."

Wesson grabbed his hat and walked outside to head to town. On the drive over, he continued to go over everything that led up to firing the two men but couldn't narrow down which one it could be. Hell, it might not be either one of them, but it was all they had right now. Hopefully the sheriff could get a confession out of one of them.

When he pulled up in front of the office, he was relieved to see that the sheriff's SUV was parked in the lot. He hadn't thought about what he'd do if the other man was out on a call. Wait he supposed.

The receptionist smiled when he walked in.

"Hey there, Wesson. How are you doing?" she asked.

"Hey, Jill. Fine. Is the sheriff available? I need to talk to him," he said.

"Just a minute and I'll check."

Wesson waited as she picked up the phone. She spoke into it while he looked around the small room.

"You can go on back, Wesson. He'll see you." Jill waved him behind the counter where the sheriff's office was located.

Wesson walked through the swinging gate and strode toward the sheriff's office. The other man stood and held out his hand when Wesson entered the room.

"Good to see you, Wesson. What can I do for you?" he asked.

"I know you're stretched thin with everything you've got going on, so I've been thinking about who would possibly shoot darts at our animals and now Jessie. I've narrowed down a list of disgruntled ex-employees that all of the affected ranches have fired in the last few years. There are two men we all have in common," he said.

"That's a good idea. I was going to suggest that the next time I talked to you but have been so damn busy that I haven't called you. What did you come up with?" the sheriff asked.

"Matthew Kirkpatrick and Sammy Jones. Both men were angry that we fired them and have been fired from the other ranches, as well. Another thing we figured out is that all of the ranches affected are into sharing their woman. This could be a hate crime," Wesson told him.

"Funny. I hadn't put that together. You are in a relationship with Jessie, the new school teacher. That's a good connection, but it opens up the field for more people to look at," the other man said.

"What do you think? Could it be someone who hates people who prefer ménage relationships?" Wesson asked.

"It's possible. There have been instances where some of the men around here have made it more than clear they don't like it. Of course there are a lot of women, as well. I honestly wouldn't think it would be a woman, but it is a possibility. There's no law that says women can't be criminals," the sheriff said.

"I hadn't even considered it could be a woman. Doesn't seem right to suspect one," Wesson said.

"I know, but women can be very vindictive. They can be just as much a fanatic as a man."

"I guess you're right." It didn't sit well with Wesson that a woman could be their culprit.

"I'll do some digging into the background of these two men you've given me. Maybe something will pop out about them that will give me a clue to if one of them is involved. After that I'll have a talk with them. It's not much to go on though."

"I know. But we have to start somewhere, and I figured those two men were good candidates."

"I'll pay them a visit and see what turns up," the sheriff said.

"I'm going to comb our ranch for anything he might have left behind in hopes it will help find this bastard. I'll give you a call if I come up with anything," Wesson said.

"You do that."

"Any luck with locating who might have bought a dart gun or tranquilizer gun?" Wesson asked.

"Not around here. I have a long list of names to go over from the surrounding cities. You'd be surprised how many are sold. If he got it online, there's no way to track him down that way. We don't have the resources for that," he said.

"Anything we can do to help, just say the word," Wesson said.

"Right now, all you can do is keep your eyes open. I just hope whoever this is doesn't escalate to using something more serious before we catch him."

Wesson shook the man's hand and left to head home. He had a lot to do before sunset. The ranch was huge, but he'd concentrate first on the surroundings of where Jessie had been shot. The bastard would have been fairly close according to what he'd learned about dart guns. Of course, he might be using a tranquilizer gun instead. That would mean a hell of a lot more land to search.

The sheriff had said that they could have purchased either one online, so narrowing the field down using that hadn't gotten them anywhere. No one sold them in the general vicinity. He was a little discouraged that the search in the surrounding cities hadn't kicked out someone from their town, but the sheriff was still checking the names. Maybe he'd get lucky. Right now they could use all the luck they could get.

Wesson drove home and saddled up his horse to begin searching for any clues he could find. He started with the surrounding tree line and worked his way out. He was just about to give up when he found footprints in the dry ground behind some brush and rocks about two hundred yards from where Jessie had been shot.

He was careful not to disturb the prints and scoured the area for any other clues. There were no cigarette butts, candy wrappers, or anything that would connect someone to the crime. The shoe prints were all that he could locate in the vicinity. He pulled out his phone to call the sheriff but found that he had no cell service. Cursing, he prayed the prints wouldn't get messed up before he could get the other man out there. Wesson urged his horse into a run to call the sheriff about his find.

* * * *

Jessie breathed a sigh of relief when she dropped her keys on the little table by the door and tossed her bag on the island in her kitchen.

Another school week finished. She loved teaching, but by the end of the week, she was ready for some downtime. The kids were so full of energy that it wore her out just being around them.

Today she'd had to really work to keep them focused. The promise of the weekend had them all distracted. Heck, she'd been just as distracted. The promise of being outdoors and having dinner with the guys was more than enough to make her lose focus a time or two. That hadn't helped keep the kids in line.

She kicked off her shoes and walked to the fridge to pour herself a Diet Coke. The first sip went a long ways to clearing her head of the jumbled thoughts of school. The second sip helped her relax enough she felt like doing something other than collapsing in a chair and vegging for a few hours.

Instead, she changed into jeans and a T-shirt then grabbed her garden gloves, shoving her hands into them. She walked outside on her front porch and looked around to see what she wanted to do. The sight of her leaf-covered front yard gave her the perfect idea of how to work off the restlessness churning inside of her. She'd spend an hour raking leaves. The exercise would do her good and help her sleep when she went to bed.

By the time she'd gotten the front yard leaf free, she was exhausted. Her muscles burned from the effort it had taken to fill the four bags she sat on the edge of the yard to be picked up when they ran the first of next week. She looked forward to a hot shower.

She looked around and shivered. For the last twenty minutes or so she'd felt as if someone had been staring at her. Looking around, she didn't see anyone and there were no telltale signs that one of her neighbors was spying out their windows at her. Jessie really didn't think any of her neighbors had a reason to watch her.

Looking across the street she wondered if old Mrs. Magillicutty had been looking out her living room window, but the curtains were drawn, and they didn't move as she stared at the other house.

Jessie shook off the feeling and chalked it up to how quiet the neighborhood seemed. She'd expected there would be other people out working in their yard, but no one had ventured outside. The sun was just about to set, and the growing darkness seemed ominous.

She smiled at her handiwork and pulled off the gloves before returning the rake to the shed out back. Despite the uneasy feeling she was being watched, it always felt good to do something around the house to make it look nicer. She'd tackle the backyard in the morning.

Her cell phone was ringing when she walked back inside. She grabbed it and hit Answer.

"Hello?"

"Hey, Jessie. How are you doing?" Cole's voice greeted her.

"I'm doing fine. I just finished raking leaves," she told him.

"It's nearly dark out. You should be careful after dark, sweet thing. I don't want anything to happen to you."

"I'm careful. It wasn't full dark when I finished. What are you doing?" she asked.

"Talking to the prettiest woman I know."

"Seriously, how is ranch life?" she asked.

"Fine. I've been doing paperwork, and Wesson's been out roaming the range," he said, the smile evident in his voice.

"Well, I've had a great week with the kids, but I'm sure glad to have a break. They're exhausting," she said.

"I can imagine. I don't think I'd have the patience to try and teach them anything worth knowing," Cole said.

"You could teach them about ranching. That would be a good idea. Ranching is such a big part of the area that learning more about it might help some of the guys to consider it when they get out of school."

"Don't leave out the women. There are plenty of women who choose to work on a ranch," he pointed out.

"True. I shouldn't have left them out."

"I'd be satisfied if some of the kids would want to make some extra money and work after school. Don't get many kids wanting to work anymore. Parents give them such generous allowances that they don't feel the need to take on an after-school job anymore," Cole said.

"That is too bad. Working helps build a sense of responsibility."

"Yeah. There's not enough of that in the youth of today. I bet you have a hard time getting them to do their homework, don't you?" he said.

"Yes. I do. I have to make it a larger part of their grades to get them to do it. Otherwise some of them would settle for a passing grade without finishing it and turning it in. I'm nicer than some of the other teachers. I only give them homework two days a week," she said.

"We're looking forward to dinner with you tomorrow night," Cole told her, changing the subject.

"I'm looking forward to it, too," she admitted.

"How about we pick you up around five," he said.

"I can drive out. There's no need for you to drive into town just to pick me up."

"We want to," Cole said.

"I don't get it, but fine. You can pick me up."

"Great. Wesson wants to talk to you. I'm going to put you on speaker phone," Cole told her.

"Hi, babe. How are you doing?" Wesson asked.

"Good. I hear you've been out riding the range. Herding the cows?" she asked.

"Something like that. I can't wait to see you tomorrow night. I'm actually doing most of the cooking tomorrow," Wesson said.

"Should I be afraid? Maybe call the fire department to be on guard?" she teased.

"No need. I'm grilling steaks. I'm safe working the grill. I make a mean steak. Cole's doing the potatoes, and we're both going to chop up the salad," Wesson said.

"Steak sounds wonderful. I can't wait," she said.

"We'll watch a movie afterwards. Any preference?" Cole asked her.

"Surprise me. Just no blood-and-guts horror movies. I have to come home at some point, and I don't want to dream about some slasher coming to get me," she told them.

"Right. No horror movies. Not a problem," Wesson said.

"We'll let you go, darling," Cole said. "Sweet dreams."

"Night, beautiful," Wesson added.

"Good night, guys. I'll see you tomorrow," she said.

When they hung up, Jessie had the feeling that they were wanting to say something more, but maybe that was just wishful thinking on her part. Surely they couldn't already be in love with her. She was barely allowing herself to feel that feeling. She hadn't admitted it to herself either. Would they ever say the words? Jessie wasn't sure, but she hoped it wasn't going to be one-sided.

She undressed and stepped into the shower to wash away the grime from raking leaves. Once she'd thoroughly washed every inch of her body and shampooed her hair, Jessie prepared for bed. She'd read a while then, once she was sufficiently relaxed, she'd call it a night and hopefully drift off despite the excitement she felt at seeing the guys again.

Chapter Fourteen

Jessie checked herself in front of the full-length mirror on the back of her bathroom door for the third time. She couldn't believe how nervous she was. It wasn't like it was her first date with the guys, but she wanted to look her best.

She'd chosen navy blue slacks and a pale blue blouse. She'd brushed her hair until it shown and applied just enough makeup to accent her eyes and give her cheeks a little color. She refreshed her lip gloss since she'd already licked it off. It was ridiculous to be this jumpy. She'd already been out with them enough times she shouldn't feel this nervous.

To make matters worse, her panties were already wet just thinking about them. If she fretted much longer, she'd have to change her panties before they'd even arrived. Even her breasts ached just thinking about them. They had her in knots while she waited on five and for them to pick her up.

She couldn't help that she was so attracted to them. They were good-looking men who could do strange things to her libido. Jessie squeezed her legs together in hopes it would alleviate the ache there. No such luck.

The sound of the doorbell made her jump. She quickly walked into the living room and checked to see who it was before she opened the door. Smiling, she pulled it open to reveal Cole standing there waiting on her.

"Hey there, beautiful. Are you ready to go?"

"Let me get my purse and I'll be ready." She strode to the island separating the kitchen from the living area and picked up her shoulder bag.

"I love that outfit. It looks great on you," he said.

"Thanks. Where's Wesson?" she asked as she closed and locked her door.

"He's working on steaks. He has this complicated marinade that he uses and needed to be there to flip the steaks at some special point he swears works." Cole winked at her. "I don't know what he puts in it, but the steaks are always damn good."

"I can't wait. I worked up an appetite today."

"What did you do all day?" he asked.

"Worked in the yard."

"I noticed all the bags sitting at the edge of the street. Did you do all that by yourself?" he asked.

"Yep. Raked the backyard, weeded the flower beds, and swept off the front and back porch and deck. I was so ready for a shower when I finished, and now I'm famished."

"Good thing we got big steaks. Hope there will be enough to fill you up," he teased.

She smiled over at him as he backed out of the drive. "I'm sure between the potato, the salad, and the steak I'll be fine."

He chuckled. "Then there's dessert."

"Did you make dessert?" she asked, widening her eyes.

"No, but I bought a pie from the bakery. Figured you'd enjoy a piece of apple pie with ice cream after dinner has settled."

"You've figured right. That sounds delicious."

They made small-talk until Cole pulled into the drive leading to their place. She always loved how warm and inviting the place seemed. Even in the fading light, it held an air of home to it.

After Cole helped her down, Wesson met them at the edge of the back deck where he'd obviously been tending to the grill. He swung her into his arms and planted a quick kiss on her lips.

There goes my lip gloss.

She smiled up at him anyway. "Hey, Wesson. I hear you've got a secret recipe for your steak. Can't wait to taste it."

"I see Cole's been blabbing. Come on inside. I just opened a bottle of wine. Want a glass?" he asked.

"I'd love a glass."

"I'll get it for you. Sit outside with Wesson while I get it." Cole gave her hand a squeeze before going inside.

"How has work been for you this week?" Wesson asked.

"Good but exhausting. I was telling Cole that some of them are lazy about homework, so I have to make it a big part of their grade to get them to do it."

"That's not unusual. I remember Cole and I hated doing it, too. Mom and Dad had to threaten to ground us to get us to do it every afternoon. We wanted to be on horseback more than we wanted good grades," he admitted.

"I suppose it's nothing new then," she said with a smile.

"Here you go." Cole handed her a glass then passed Wesson a beer. "How long before the steaks will be done?"

"You said the potatoes will be ready at six, so I'll put them on in another few minutes." Wesson turned to Jessie. "How do you like your steak cooked?"

"Medium is fine with me," she told them.

"That works out. We like ours medium rare. I'll put yours on a few minutes before I add ours. That will make them all ready at the same time," Wesson said.

"Don't you love sitting out here at night?" Jessie asked, looking up at the sky.

She loved how she could see thousands of stars above her. Without the lights of the town or a big city, they were bright in the night sky.

"We usually sit out here with a beer every night," Cole admitted.

"I'd love to do that. My deck is too close to the street lights to really be able to see many stars. Still, it's better than when I was in a larger city while I was at school," she said.

"You're welcome out here to star gaze anytime you want to come," Wesson said.

"Thanks."

"I'm going to check the potatoes. They should be just about done," Cole said.

She watched him stride across the deck and disappear inside the house. She couldn't help but admire his ass with the way he filled out his jeans. With his broad shoulders and narrow waist, he was heaven to look at.

"Ogling Cole's body?" Wesson asked, wrapping his arms around her.

Jessie jerked her eyes up to him. She was embarrassed at being caught staring at the man's physique.

"Hey, you're turning red. There's no reason to be embarrassed about it. I've seen you look at me like that, too. Really turns me on that you think we're good-looking," Wesson said.

"I can't help it, but it's embarrassing to get caught looking," she admitted.

"Nonsense. How's the wine?" Wesson asked.

"Good. It will go perfectly with the steaks. I'm starved. Can't wait to eat," she admitted.

"Been busy today?" he asked.

Jessie filled him in on her day. Cole returned with a smile on his face. She enjoyed seeing both men smile. They were good-looking without the smile, but when they grinned, it gave them mischievous looks that would put her kids to shame.

"Time to put the steaks on, Wesson. The potatoes are just about ready. I've got the table set, as well," he said.

"Great." Wesson walked over to the grill and flipped the top up.

"Come on inside. You can watch as I get out the salad and stuff for the potatoes," Cole said.

Jessie followed the other man into the kitchen and watched as he set the salad on the table and pulled the butter out of the fridge. Then he added sour cream and salt and pepper shakers. Lastly, he pulled out the potatoes and all but tossed them on the plates as he growled out, *Ouch, ouch* with each potato he picked up.

She couldn't help but laugh at him when he sucked his fingers.

"You should have used a pot holder to pick them up, silly."

"Forgot about that," he admitted.

"Your fingers are going to be tender the rest of the night," she warned.

"Won't stop me from touching you, sweet thing. I can promise you that."

Once again she could feel her face heat up, which drew a soft chuckle from Cole's mouth. Before he could say anything more, Wesson walked in with the steaks.

"Let's eat, guys," he said.

They all sat down and busied themselves with fixing their salads and potatoes the way they liked. The men talked about what they'd been up to all week then insisted she tell them about her days at school. They hadn't appeared the least bored by her relating the antics of her students. It felt good to have someone to talk to about work for a change.

"Sounds like you have a good time despite the challenges," Cole said.

"I do. I love teaching and for the most part, the students are challenging and fun to be around," she admitted.

They continued talking, moving to the kitchen to put the dishes in the dishwasher and everything else in the refrigerator. Jessie helped despite their protesting. She wasn't raised to leave dishes for the host to wash. No, they weren't hand-washing them, but still.

I just want to be around them is all. I might as well face it. I've fallen for them.

She could finally admit it to herself, but she had no idea how they felt or if she could continue in a threesome relationship. There just seemed to be too many roadblocks for them. Despite her friend's assurance that her job was safe, Jessie still worried. The assistant principal could still make things hard for her even if the school board sided with her. Then there was the city itself. Would she be treated any differently because of her decision to be with two men?

Whoa. She was getting ahead of herself. They hadn't said anything about making their relationship into anything other than the casual one they presently had. Yes, she was intimate with them, but just because she felt more for them didn't mean they felt the same way.

I need to be prepared for them to eventually break it off. I might not be what they're looking for in a woman. It's only been a month.

One month hadn't prevented her from falling in love with them though. She loved each of them just as much, though differently. Wesson was serious and intense in how he looked at her, making her feel like the only person in a room worth his attention. She loved how he moved as if the world was his for the taking. She sure as heck was. Cole was more laid back and easy to be around. She loved how he smiled so that it reached his light blue eyes making them twinkle.

"What has that serious expression on your face?" Cole asked as they walked into the living room.

"Oh, nothing. Just thinking about school," she lied.

"No more thinking about work. Let's watch a movie and relax," Cole said.

Wesson scrolled through Netflix and chose a movie they could all appreciate. Jessie sat between them, each of them holding one of her hands. Cole drew tiny circles with his fingers over the back of one hand while Wesson stroked the back of her other. She was so aware of them as men that she had trouble following the storyline of the movie. They were monopolizing her entire attention and didn't even seem to be aware of it.

Jessie had them pause the movie to run to the bathroom. While she was there she tried to get her galloping libido under control. They were seducing her just as surely as if they'd been kissing and touching her more intimately.

When she returned, they started the movie again and settled back as if nothing was going on. Maybe it was all her and they weren't even aware of what they were doing to her. Jessie knew without a doubt that she would have to watch herself or she'd throw herself on them the minute the movie was over. She wanted them with a single-minded determination that scared her.

I'm so screwed.

* * * *

"That was a great movie," Jessie said.

"Yeah. Can't go wrong with a good suspense movie," Wesson said.

"As long as it wasn't a cheesy romance," Cole teased her.

"Hey, don't knock romance movies. They're great for girls' night," she told them.

"I'm all for a little romance," Wesson said, leaning closer to her and capturing her gaze with his much darker ones.

Jessie shivered from head to toe at the intensity of it. She couldn't help but look at his mouth as he drew closer. Then he was kissing her as if he'd crawl inside of her. She couldn't stop her answering need from returning the kiss. She felt Cole behind her, wrapping his arms around her and massaging her breasts with his hands.

"You're so damn sexy," Cole breathed into her ear.

His warm breath tickled when he sucked on her earlobe before kissing a line down her neck to her shoulder, nuzzling aside her collar to nip at her skin.

Jessie moaned into Wesson's mouth. He explored every inch of it with his tongue, lapping at her as if he would drink her down. When he pulled back, it left her breathless and hot. Her skin itched to be out of her clothes. She couldn't explain it, only that she needed to be naked between the two men.

Cole turned her head to allow him to reach her mouth with his. He sucked on her bottom lip then thrust his tongue inside her so that their tongues tangled before he slowly pulled away.

"We need to take this to the bedroom before we go any farther. The couch is no place for what I want to do with you," Wesson said, his voice deep and raspy.

Jessie gazed up into his face that held a seriousness that both thrilled her and made her edgy. She wanted him focused on her, but the look he was giving her promised all sorts of things. Dirty amazing things.

She stood when Cole pulled her to her feet before leading her by one hand to the back of the house where the bedrooms were. They urged her into the master bedroom, stopping just inside the door to kiss her once more. Cole began unbuttoning her blouse as Wesson knelt at her feet to pull off her shoes. Then he knelt up to unfasten her pants and pull them down her legs.

Cole had her blouse unfastened and was pulling it off her shoulders. He paused and kissed each inch of skin he bared, drawing it all out until Jessie was ready to scream at him to pull it off already. Then he worked on her bra.

"Love the matching underwear, darling. That light blue matches what you had on over it," Cole said.

"I love her out of all of it even more," Wesson said as he had her step out of her underwear next.

"I'm naked, and both of you are still dressed. I want your clothes off, too," she said in a breathy voice.

"We'll take off our shirts, but the jeans stay on, or we'll never get to worship this amazing body of yours. I'm so fucking hard I might take you before I get to love on you," Wesson said in a growling voice.

"Then take off your shirts so I can touch you. I want to feel your skin beneath my hands," she said.

She watched as both men toed off their boots then reached behind them to grab their T-shirts and pull them over their heads at the same time. It was like watching them strip in stereo. She couldn't stop staring at their hard, muscled bodies as they stood in front of her with grins on their faces. She scowled at them.

"Don't look so full of yourselves."

"Can't help it when you look at us like you want to jump our bones," Wesson said with a wide grin.

"The look on your face has my dick straining at my zipper to get out. I swear I'm hard enough to pound concrete," Cole told her.

"Look at her, man. She's perfect," Wesson said as he reached to stroke one finger down her arm. "I want to taste her, but I can't decide where to start."

"I know where I want to start," Cole said. "Climb up on the bed, sweet thing. I want to see if you're wet for us."

Jessie felt heat creep up her neck to pool in her cheeks. She was wet. In fact, she could feel her juices coating her inner thighs. It was embarrassing how wet they got her just with a look and those amazing kisses from earlier.

She climbed on the bed and turned over to sit and watch them as they prowled toward her. They looked like big cats as they moved to stand just in front of the foot of the bed.

"Lie back, babe," Wesson said. "Let us see your pretty pussy."

Jessie lay back but didn't spread her legs. She was too shy to just spread herself like that.

She didn't have to worry that they'd get mad at her for resisting. Wesson took one ankle and Cole the other, and they pulled until she was spread out like a wishbone for their enjoyment.

"Look at how wet she is, Cole. That sweet pussy is glistening with her juices," Wesson said.

"Can't wait to lick all that juice," Cole said.

"Me, too. You can go first. I'm going to suck on her nipples. They're all pink and puckered. Bet they're just as tasty," Wesson said and climbed on the bed next to her.

Cole knelt on the floor then pulled her body toward him so that her bottom was resting at the edge of the bed. He lifted both of her legs and settled her feet on his shoulders then leaned in and inhaled her scent. Even more blood rushed to her cheeks when he did that. He was going to make her die of embarrassment. She just knew it.

"You smell like warm honey. I bet you taste just as good. Don't you, darling?" Cole leaned in and licked her slit from bottom to top.

Jessie couldn't stop the low moan that escaped her lips at the brief touch of his tongue against her nether lips. He chuckled then blew against her folds before licking at them and sucking them into his mouth.

Her attentions were divided when Wesson mounded her breasts with his hands then laved his tongue across one nipple then the other. He squeezed each breast before sucking on one puckered nipple, making her squirm even more. It was all too much with both men paying such close attention to her. She couldn't figure out where to focus, her pussy or her breasts. They were driving her crazy this way.

"Please," she moaned out.

"Please what, babe?" Wesson asked before sucking hard on her nipple.

"I don't know. It's too much," she whimpered.

"It's not enough, Jess," Cole whispered against her pussy lips.

She nearly screamed when Cole sucked on her clit before licking at her juices once more. Then he thrust two fingers deep inside her making her cry out at how good it felt to finally have something inside of her.

"That what you want, sweetheart?" Cole crooned.

"More. I need more," she cried out in a hoarse voice.

"As soon as you come, babe." Wesson twisted her nipple then nipped the other one.

"Oh, God. I'll die if I don't," she told them.

"We'll take care of you, darling," Cole said.

Then they were touching and licking and sucking and tugging on her from top to bottom. She couldn't be sure who was doing what as her body burned for them, edged closer and closer to ecstasy.

Finally, when she was sure she would combust, her orgasm washed over her like a storm-lashed beach. She cried out, and then her voice went hoarse and nothing would come out as she jerked and bucked between them. Finally they had mercy on her and pulled back. She couldn't open her eyes for long seconds as she fought to control her breathing.

"You can't imagine how amazing you look right now," Wesson whispered into her ear. "All pink and rosy from your orgasm with a fine sheen of sweat coating your body. You glow, babe. You fucking glow, and we did this to you."

"I think I died and went to heaven, but they kicked me out," she said in a raspy voice that didn't even sound like her.

"Nonsense. Someone as sweet as you they'd have kept," Cole said.

"We want you, Jessie. We want to make love to you at the same time. Can you allow us to do that?" Wesson asked.

"I—I don't know. I've never had anal sex. How is there room for both of you at one time?" she asked, nerves jumping at the idea.

"We'll fit, darling. We'll take good care of you. I promise. If you need to stop, we stop, no questions," Cole assured her.

"I want you guys, too. I'm a little scared though," she said.

"Let us get you ready and we'll take it slow," Wesson said.

"Okay."

Chapter Fifteen

Jessie wasn't sure about taking both men at the same time, but she trusted them to stop if she asked them to. They were good men and had treated her like a princess ever since she'd met them. But anal sex? At the same time as regular sex? She didn't know how it could possibly feel good for her. Still, she wanted to try. She'd read about it in her romance novels, but that was fiction, and this was real life.

"Climb up on Cole, Jessie," Wesson said. "Straddle him and take him inside of you."

Cole had laid back on the bed, his hand slowly moving up and down over his thick, hard cock. She could see the drop of pre-cum at the top before he ran the palm of his hand over the top and spread it down his erection. The sight was mesmerizing. She hesitated until he held out one hand to her.

Jessie climbed on top of him and slowly slid down the hard, silken length of him until she felt as if he were lodged in her throat. He was thick and so very hard. She squirmed as he seemed to swell inside her.

"So fucking tight," Cole rasped out.

"You feel good inside of me," she said, her voice whisper-soft as she fought to be still.

"Fuck me," Cole said. "I want to feel you glide over me, darling."

The idea of moving up and down his rigid dick made her shiver as she slowly rose up then sank down on him over and over in a slow, torturous rhythm that had both of them groaning. Then Wesson gently pushed her over so that she lay against Cole's chest. While Cole kissed her, Wesson spread something cool and greasy against her back hole. He rubbed little circles around the puckered entrance before adding more of the slick lubricant.

"I bet you're going to be tight back here, aren't you, babe?" he asked.

Jessie couldn't say anything. Cole was kissing her, and she really didn't know what to say to that anyway. Despite Cole trying to distract her, she was nervous and stiff with worry.

"Relax, babe. Nothing happens that you don't agree to. Let me get you ready. You need to let go so that you're not all rigid." Wesson massaged her ass cheeks, spreading them as he did.

She willed herself to do as he said, draping herself over Cole's chest so that her head lay over his heart. The steady beat calmed her as Wesson pressed a single finger inside her ass. He didn't go far, just an inch, before drawing back and squirting more of the liquid inside her. He pushed his finger in deeper this time and slowly moved it in and out of her until she was taking his entire finger without any trouble.

The feeling of his finger back there wasn't unpleasant at all. In fact, it felt sort of nice. Then he added more lubricant and a second finger. It pinched at first, but after a few seconds of the slow, easy rhythm he'd set, it felt good, as well. Who would have thought that there were pleasure points in her ass?

"I think you're ready, Jessie. Are you okay with me pushing my cock inside that tight ass of yours?" Wesson asked.

"I think so. I mean I want to try. What you've already done felt sort of good."

"Remember, if you need me to, I'll stop." Wesson massaged her ass cheeks as he spoke.

"Okay."

She felt him add more lubricant, and then there was more pressure than she'd felt before. Cole wrapped his arms around her back and rubbed his hands up and down her back as Wesson slowly breached her back hole with his cock. It stung then burned as he entered her. There was another moment of sharp pain, and then he was inside of her, and she felt so full she didn't know how to react.

"Are you okay?" Wesson gritted out from behind her.

He wasn't moving, and she needed him to move. With Cole inside of her at the same time, she felt as if she were choking, and the pressure was just this side of pain.

"Yes," she ground out. "But I need you to move. Do something. It's too much."

Wesson pulled back then pushed deeper inside of her as Cole pulled out. The exchange of positions as the men rubbed oversensitive nerve endings soon had her groaning with a pleasure she'd never felt before. How could something feel so good and so bad at the same time?

"Fuck, you're so tight I'm never going to last long," Wesson said in a strained voice.

"With you inside of her, I'm in the same boat," Cole said from beneath her.

"Oh, God," was all that Jessie could say.

Pleasure rolled through her as both men moved over and under her, sending waves of pleasure coursing through her body like nothing she'd ever experienced before. She actually had both of the men she loved inside of her at one time. It was a heady feeling.

"So tight, so good," Wesson hissed out.

"Are you okay, darling?" Cole asked in a husky voice.

"Yes. Don't stop. I'm close." Jessie never would have believed she could climax with both men inside of her. She'd expected it to hurt too bad for that.

Cole slid his hand between their bodies and rubbed lightly over her clit. The dual sensation of both of their bodies seesawing into her and the press of his finger against her little nub was too much. Jessie screamed out as her orgasm roared through her. It felt as if every nerve ending inside of her exploded at the same time. Pleasure engulfed her as she flew sightlessly.

After what felt like hours, Jessie came to herself with both men petting her. Cole's hands rubbed up and down her back while Wesson rubbed up and down her upper thighs. She felt him pull out and realized they'd evidently both come when she had. The pressure eased from her body when he withdrew.

"Don't move, babe. I'm going to clean you up," Wesson said.

She felt cool air brush over her ass when he moved away. She was still on top of Cole with his softening cock inside of her. She didn't want to move. She felt too good where she was.

"Are you okay?" Cole asked her.

"Um-hm." She couldn't manage much else.

Cole chuckled. "Cat got your tongue?"

"Feel good," she finally breathed out.

Then Wesson was back with a warm cloth. She should have felt embarrassed as he cleaned her up, but all she could feel at the moment was relaxed and sated. They'd pulled every bit of pleasure from her until she was limp with it.

Once Wesson was finished, Cole lifted her off of him and settled her next to him. Jessie curled over him as Wesson climbed into bed on the other side of her and spooned behind her. She couldn't believe how good she felt or how tired she was. Minutes later she felt herself drift off still in a haze of pleasure.

* * * *

Cole petted Jessie's upper back as she lightly snored. He grinned. They'd worn her out. He couldn't help but feel some pride that he'd been a part of taking care of her.

"She's exhausted," he told his brother.

"I'm about wiped myself," Wesson said.

"She felt so damn good."

"Yeah, she did. I've never felt anything like that before."

Wesson brushed a strand of Jessie's hair aside and kissed her neck. Cole kissed her forehead. She'd given them a treasure by allowing them to make love to her at the same time. He cherished it.

"I love her, Wesson. I think I've loved her since the beginning," Cole said.

"I love her, too. She's a-fucking-mazing."

"I want to tell her."

"I think it's too soon."

Cole sighed. Wesson would hold out, but Cole didn't want to. He looked over Jessie at his brother.

"I think she feels the same way. She wouldn't have given herself to us like this if she didn't feel something more," he said.

"Yeah. I know you're right, but what if she doesn't love us like we do her?" Wesson asked.

"I believe she does. I don't want to wait. She needs to know how we feel."

"But what if you're wrong?" Wesson persisted.

"I'm not. We've got to tell her."

Wesson was quiet after that. Cole knew his brother worried that she'd disappoint them. He might be the most stoic of the two of them, but he was also the most vulnerable when it came to women. He expected them to disappoint them because, in the past, they always had. Jessie was different. He was positive of that.

Cole planned on telling Jessie how he felt the next day, even if Wesson didn't. He wanted her to know how special she was and what she meant to them. She deserved to know.

"Okay, I'll tell her with you," Wesson said from the other side of the bed.

Cole had thought the other man was asleep, but he'd obviously been drifting in and out of sleep.

"Good. We'll tell her tomorrow. She's going to want to go home early to get ready for school on Monday," Cole said.

"I know. I hate for her to leave, but I know she needs to. I want her with us always. Do you think she'll move in with us if we ask her?" Wesson asked.

"I don't know."

"Do we ask her?"

"Not yet. Let her get used to us loving her first."

"Yeah. Guess you're right."

Cole smiled. Once Wesson admitted to himself, then told Jessie, he was all out in wanting to make it permanent. Still, asking her to move in with them needed to come after they asked her to marry them.

He was sure Wesson wanted to hear her say the words back to them as much as Cole wanted that. He was almost positive she felt the same way, but what if she didn't? It would hurt. It would probably devastate his brother. Was it too soon to say them? Cole didn't think so. They'd taken a big step when they'd taken her at the same time. To him it meant they were serious in the relationship. Would she see it the same way? The only way to find out was to tell her how they felt and see how she took it.

Cole kissed her forehead and looked at her lying draped over him. He loved her so damn much. He prayed that telling her how he felt wouldn't drive her away. With that last thought, he allowed himself to fall asleep.

Chapter Sixteen

Jessie woke to the scent of frying bacon and coffee. She stretched and realized she was alone in the bed. Her body felt comfortably sore. The kind of sore that spoke of amazing sex the night before. She couldn't believe she'd had both men inside of her at the same time. It seemed so naughty but, at the same time, so right.

She scooted to the edge of the bed and stood, looking for something to put on in order to follow her nose to the kitchen. She located one of the men's shirts and pulled it on. It fell to her knees. She slipped on her underwear and padded into the bathroom. Once she'd washed her face and combed her hair, Jessie shuffled toward the kitchen where she found both men. Wesson was sitting at the bar with a mug of coffee in front of him while Cole stood at the stove frying the bacon.

"Morning," Wesson said.

"Good morning," she said. "Coffee smells great." Wesson stood and walked over to the counter where he poured her a cup then handed it to her.

"How do you feel this morning?" Cole asked, turning from the stove.

"Good. I feel good," she told him.

"Hungry?" he asked.

"Starved. I can't believe I am considering that meal last night," she confessed.

"I'm making bacon and pancakes," Cole told her.

"Have a seat," Wesson said, patting the stool next to him.

She climbed up and sipped her coffee. It was delicious.

They talked about nothing in particular all through breakfast. She loved that the conversation didn't seem the least bit awkward after their night together. She'd been worried they'd be distant and withdrawn. She'd worried for nothing.

Once they'd cleaned up the dishes, the two men urged her into the living room where they set her between them on the couch. She expected they'd turn on the TV, but instead, they each took one of her hands in theirs.

"We want to tell you something," Cole said.

"What?" she asked, a little apprehensive now.

"We love you, Jessie," Cole said.

Of all the things she'd expected him to say, it hadn't been that. She felt relief and surprise rush over her like a cool spring wind. They loved her. They really loved her. Jessie smiled up at Cole then Wesson. She was about to tell them that she loved them, as well, when Wesson pulled her into his arms and kissed her. It was a desperate kiss full of need. Then Cole was pulling her toward him with a kiss full of promise.

She finally recovered enough to tell them how she felt. "I love both of you, too. I was afraid to say it, that it was too soon, but I do. I love you both."

Both men heaved out a breath and fought to hold her. She giggled as they wrestled her between them.

"Easy, guys. One at a time. I feel like a pull toy." She laughed.

"Sorry," Cole said. He leaned back.

Wesson didn't seem willing to let her go. It made her smile. She had two men who looked like Greek gods who said they loved her. It hardly seemed real.

They cuddled on the couch and watched a movie before Jessie reluctantly said she needed to go to get ready for school the next day.

"We'll call you later," Wesson said. "I'll drive you home."

"I love you," Cole told her as they stood in the open door of the truck.

"I love you, too. I'll talk to you later," she said.

Wesson seemed reluctant to let her leave. She knew he was wanting to say more, but held back. She couldn't imagine what it might be. Then Cole moved him out of the way and closed the door.

Jessie waved to him as Wesson backed around in the drive and drove toward the main road. Immediately she felt a sense of loss at leaving. She wanted to stay longer, but she had things to do. Although she'd done most of her chores before going over to the guys' house, she still needed to put away her laundry and pick out what she would wear the next day. None of that seemed all that important now.

This is crazy. I can't stay there all the time. I have to come home sometime and tend to my own house.

Still, she felt the loss as they pulled into her drive. Jessie smiled as Wesson opened her door and helped down from the truck.

"Remember to lock up and have a good day at work tomorrow."

"I had a great time, Wesson."

He cupped her face in his big hands and kissed her. It was a chaste kiss by their standards, but it affected her in a big way. Her heart stuttered in her chest even as the breath left her lungs. He smiled and gave her a little push toward her door.

"Go on inside, Jessie," he said.

She'd just stepped into the house when her phone dinged letting her know she had a text message. She pulled her cell out and smiled. It was from Cole wanting to be sure she'd made it home safely. Jessie texted him back that she had and wished him a good night.

Jessie till couldn't believe that both men loved her. She'd been so worried that they wouldn't feel the same about her as she felt about them, and now they'd confessed that they did. It felt so good. She fairly danced around the house as she got ready for school. When she'd finally settled down for the night, her phone dinged again. She checked the message to find it was from Cole wishing her a good night. She smiled and texted back the same to him and Wesson.

She was sure she'd dream about the two men when she finally fell asleep. Knowing they loved her was the best feeling in the world.

* * * *

School breezed by the next few weeks as she concentrated on the kids and her lesson plans. The men called her every day after work to find out how her day went. She grew to depend on those calls, as being away from them had been harder than she'd realized it would be. Now that they'd all confessed their feelings, she wanted to be with them more and more. Where would all of it lead?

They'd missed having their Saturday the last weekend since she'd gone with Brenda to help her pick out her wedding dress. They'd spent the day in the city choosing shoes, lingerie, and discussing the wedding reception. Jessie had had an amazing time, but she'd missed the guys.

By the next Friday she was anxious to see them, but they'd planned for Saturday afternoon. She'd suggested going riding, but the guys had vetoed that idea since the person who'd shot her was still out there somewhere. She shivered at the thought of her two men outside with the bastard still at large.

She and Brenda planned on meeting up at the pizza place that night to catch up. She couldn't wait to tell her the news. She was sure the other woman would be happy for her. Her only worry was that Brenda would start planning a wedding for her. That was still down the road if it happened at all. Secretly, she hoped it would, but she couldn't help but wonder who she'd marry if they asked.

"So how was your week?" Brenda asked.

"Long, but good. What about yours?" Jessie asked.

"Same here. My dress came in, and it was the wrong color. I ordered candlelight, and it came in off-white," the other woman said.

"Oh my God. What did you do?"

"I sent it back and told them they better get it right and put a rush on it. I was so upset."

"I can't believe you didn't call me. I know you were devastated to see it."

"I didn't want to bother you about it."

"That's what friends are for. That's what your maid of honor is for," Jessie reminded her.

"I know. I know."

"Are you getting wedding jitters already?" Jessie teased.

"No. Yes. I don't know." Brenda waved her hands in the air. Tears glistened in her eyes.

"Hey, what's wrong?" Jessie reached over and took one of the other woman's hands.

"I don't know. I'm just worried I'm making a mistake."

"Why would you think that?" Jessie asked.

"We've only known each other for eight months. What if he decides he doesn't really love me?"

"Are you kidding me? He's head over hills in love with you. The way he looks at you is proof enough. You're his world, Brenda."

"Really? You think so?"

"I know so. I can see it when he looks at you. What started all of this?" Jessie asked.

"I've been trying to get him to help make choices about the wedding, but he doesn't seem all that interested in it," Brenda said.

"Brenda, most men don't want to have anything to do with planning one. It's a woman thing, not a guy thing. They could care less about colors and flowers. You know that."

"I know, I know. I guess I'm overly sensitive with everything coming up so soon. I'm afraid I won't be ready, that I won't have everything done by the time it gets here." Brenda leaned back when the waitress brought their drinks.

"Tell me what you need me to do. I haven't done much to help you. That's not right. I'm supposed to help and take some of the pressure off you." Jessie felt guilty. She'd been so caught up in dating Cole and Wesson that she'd neglected her best friend.

"You've been wonderful. I don't think I could have gotten through this without you. There really isn't all that much left to do. I'm just panicking. That's all."

"Nonsense. Do you need me to work on the reception some more? Have you hired the musicians?" she asked.

"That's all done. I actually got Steve to help me with that part. He knew a band he liked and asked them to play at the reception," Brenda told her.

"Great. See, he's helped. I know you've already picked out the flowers, but what about the decorations for the reception? Is everything we picked out turning out okay? Has any of it come in yet?" Jessie asked.

They discussed the reception up until their pizza came then concentrated on eating with a word here and there about colors and food. Jessie was antsy to tell her friend her good news but hesitated since Brenda was having a mini-crisis. It could wait.

By the time they'd finished eating, Brenda seemed back to her old self, laughing and smiling as they exchanged work stories.

"What about you and the guys? How is everything going between you three?" Brenda asked.

"Really good." She debated about telling the other woman about what they'd told her, but she was so excited she couldn't keep it in.

"They told me they love me," she blurted out.

Brenda's face exploded into a smile so bright Jessie was sure it rivaled hers.

"Oh my God! That's perfect. Did you tell them back? Sure you did. I know you love them."

"I did. I can't believe they said it though. It still feels like a dream," she admitted.

"Do they call you during the week?" Brenda asked.

"Every night," Jessie admitted.

"That's love. They can't stand to be away from you. That's wonderful news. I can't believe you didn't tell me right away," the other woman gushed.

"I was too worried about you. My news could wait." Jessie patted the other woman's hand.

"Have they asked you to marry them yet?" Brenda asked.

"No. It's too soon. I don't expect them to do that yet. I mean I hope they will one day, but it's too soon. We haven't known each other very long at all," Jessie said.

"Long enough for them to fall for you. This is wonderful news."

They talked for another thirty minutes, and then they agreed that it was time to go. Brenda said that Steve was supposed to come by later that night. She seemed much more relaxed and happy after their talk.

"Don't forget that the fitting is next Saturday at ten a.m.," Brenda said.

"I won't. I can't wait to see everyone all dressed up."

They said good-bye and parted ways outside in the parking lot. Jessie drove home feeling light and relaxed. Brenda had been her best friend since grade school. They'd always gotten along and were so much alike that she felt like a sister to her even more than her best friend. Seeing Brenda distressed over the wedding had worried her, but now that the crisis was past, Jessie thought about how she'd feel if the guys asked her to marry them. Would she get as frazzled as her friend?

I'm jumping ahead of myself. They might not ask me. They may just want to keep things like they are.

That worried her for a few minutes. She brushed it away. She couldn't marry two men, so they might not want to get married at all. They might just want to move in together. That would mean she'd move in with them since they had a ranch to run.

Thinking of that made her wonder about the person who'd shot her and how the guys didn't want her out riding with them. They were worried that she'd be shot again. Why would someone want to shoot people, much less live stock? It was sick and wrong in so many ways.

Jessie brushed the thought aside and relaxed in her favorite chair to read before bed. She'd just about decided to head to bed when her phone rang. She smiled as Wesson's name greeted her when she picked up her phone.

"Hey, beautiful," he said by way of greeting.

"Hey, you. How are you and Cole doing?" she asked.

"Good. What about you?"

"Great. I miss you two."

"We miss you, too. How was your diner with Brenda?" he asked.

Jessie glossed over their meal together, leaving out the other woman's worries and talked about her wedding plans instead. To her surprise, Wesson was more interested in it than she would have believed.

"What about the guy who's been shooting at the cattle and horses? Any word on who it is?" she asked.

"Not yet. The sheriff is working on trying to find out who it is."

"I hope he does soon. I want to go horseback riding with you two again. I really enjoyed it."

"We want to go, too, but not until this asshole is caught. It's too dangerous. We're not risking your life like that." Wesson's voice had grown hard.

"Do you think they'll ever catch him? Has he shot anything else lately?"

"They'll catch him. But no. He hasn't as far as we know."

"I just can't understand anyone who'd shoot defenseless animals. That's just cruel," she said.

"He shot you, Jessie. He obviously doesn't care about anyone but himself." Wesson's voice had grown cold.

Jessie could hear Cole on the other end saying something. Wesson spoke with the other man then sighed.

"Cole wants to talk to you. Hold on," Wesson said with some reluctance.

"Hey, darling. Don't let Wesson dampen your mood. We're both worried about you and don't want to see you hurt again," Cole told her.

"I know. I worry about you guys out working, as well. He could shoot one of you, you know." Jessie wanted him to know she worried about them, as well.

"We're fine, hon. So are you up to going out Saturday night?" he asked.

"Sounds great. Where are we going?"

"How about to eat fish at the fish house over in Searcy?"

"That sounds yummy. I love fish."

"Great. It's a date."

They talked for a few more minutes then hung up with Jessie feeling on top of the world. They'd both ended the call by telling her they loved her. She couldn't stop her face from splitting into a broad smile the rest of the night. She refused to let anything dampen her happiness. Not even the bastard who was still out there preventing her from riding with her men.

Chapter Seventeen

"Well, the two men you gave me are clear. They were both working when the attack on Jessie happened," the sheriff told Wesson and Cole.

"Are you sure? Was there any way one of them could have slipped away?" Wesson asked.

"I'm sure. They were both working for a ranch almost seventy-five miles from here and were surrounded by the other ranch hands as they rounded up some cattle for sale. No way either one of them could have been here from that far away," the sheriff said.

"What about the drug? Have you figured out how he got it?" Wesson asked.

"I checked with the doctors surrounding us, and no one is missing any of their supply. It's possible he could have gotten it some other way, but I haven't figured out how at this point," the sheriff said.

"Damn. We're back to square one," Wesson said.

"Don't get too involved with this, guys. It's a law enforcement job. Not yours," the sheriff said.

"The bastard shot Jessie. She's our woman. There's no way we're not getting involved. We're already involved," Wesson said with vehemence.

"I don't want you guys mixed up in this. It's dangerous and could jeopardize the investigation," the other man said.

"We're not standing by while someone takes potshots at our ranch and our woman," Wesson said again.

"Damnit, Wesson. Don't make me arrest you for interfering with an investigation."

"I'm not interfering, just keeping my eyes open," Wesson said.

Cole nudged him. "We're not going to do anything that will risk letting this guy get away."

"See that you don't," the sheriff said then walked back to his vehicle and climbed in.

After the sheriff drove off, Wesson cursed and jabbed his hands on his hips. They were nowhere with catching this guy. Who the hell could it be? Why was he doing it in the first place? He couldn't help but believe it was someone who didn't like the threesomes cropping up all over town.

"What are you thinking?" Cole asked him.

"I still think it has something to do with our lifestyle. The only ranches that have been hit are those with a threesome relationship or that are open about wanting one," he said.

"I agree with you on that. The problem is, how do we figure out who it is? There have been several people who've been public about their disapproval."

"I think it's going to be someone who hasn't spoken up in public about it. They're too cowardly to be obvious about it," Wesson said.

"Maybe you're right, but that doesn't get us any closer to figuring out who it is."

"I know you're right, but it's the best I can come up with."

Wesson wanted to approach everyone in town and demand to know how they felt about their dating Jessie but knew it wouldn't do any good and would only stir things up with people who didn't feel one way or another about their relationship. It was a crazy idea at best. But he couldn't stand to do nothing. There just had to be something they could do.

"I have a feeling the only way this guy is going to get caught is when he messes up, and that might not be in time to save someone from being seriously injured or worse," Wesson said.

"I'm afraid you're right. If he's careful, he could still be out there this time next year." Cole jabbed his hands in the pockets of his jeans. "I've got the hands keeping their eyes open for anything suspicious, but I don't expect them to see or find anything. Let's just hope he's stopped screwing around and has given up. Maybe the sheriff poking around has him scared and he's stopped."

"You don't believe that any more than I do. He's still out there plotting his next move. It's only a matter of time before he strikes again," Wesson said.

"You're probably right, but I'm hoping I'm right instead."

"I'm almost afraid for Jessie to even come home with us on the weekends. How do we know he won't come closer to the house and shoot her while she's here?" Wesson asked.

"I don't think he's going to risk getting too close."

"I hope you're right about that. I don't want anything else happen to Jessie. That took years off my life seeing her lying there unconscious." Wesson turned toward the house. "I need a beer. Want one?"

"Yeah. That sounds pretty damn good right about now." Cole followed him inside.

"Is it too soon to think about asking Jessie to marry us?" Wesson asked.

Cole stopped just inside the kitchen and stared at him.

"What?" Wesson asked.

"You're talking about marriage. That's not like you."

"Why?"

"Because you're always the one to put the brakes on in our relationships," Cole said.

"I love Jessie. I don't want to do that with her. I want her here with us for more than a night or two here and there."

"I'm with you on that, but I'd feel better if this guy were caught before we ask her to marry us. Having her here full time just increases the chance that she could get hurt again," Cole said.

Wesson knew his brother was right. With the bastard still at large, having her at the ranch all the time outside of her job increased the chances he'd shoot her again. And the next time might not be with a tranquilizer. No, Cole was right. They needed to hold off on asking her for now. It grated on him though.

"You're right. I don't want to take any chances with her life. Doesn't stop me from wanting her near us though." Wesson turned up his beer and drained it before tossing the empty bottle into the recycling bin.

"I feel the same way. She makes me smile even when I've had a tough-as-shit day," Cole said.

"Yeah. That about sums it up," Wesson agreed.

* * * *

Jessie stood outside the cafeteria watching the kids file in to eat. She smiled at the ones who called out to her and nodded at them. She loved her job, but there were days when she got frustrated with the troublemakers. Today, two of her older boys were disruptive in class by being sarcastic about the reading they'd had for class that morning. It was obvious they hadn't bothered to read it, but they'd trashed it as if they had.

"This is all stupid. What does some old-as-hell story have to do with the world today?" one of them had asked.

"It's all just dumb stories about lame people who act like wimps," the other boy had said.

The entire class had erupted into chaos, choosing sides and turning her normally quiet classroom into a battleground of sorts. It had taken her the rest of the period to calm everyone down and a trip to the principal's office with the two unruly teens.

Now, as she stood just inside the doorway of the cafeteria, the assistant principal strode up with a sour expression on his face. Jessie knew trouble when she saw it.

"You seem to be having a hard time keeping your class in order, Jessie," he said by way of a greeting.

"There will always be a couple of kids who act out. Literature isn't something most boys enjoy," she said.

"They don't respect you. I wonder why that is?" he asked.

"What do you mean?"

"The kids looks up to us to direct them in life. We're supposed to be morally good adults so that the kids will grow up with strong morals and a good work ethic," he said.

"What is that supposed to mean? I have a great work ethic and good morals. What are you suggesting?" she asked again.

"Dating two men isn't good morals, Jessie. You're teaching these kids that they don't have to follow the rules. That's not a good thing to teach young impressionable teenagers when they're already exploring their sexuality," he said.

"My personal life doesn't have any bearing on my teaching skills. None of the kids have even mentioned who I'm dating in class. I seriously doubt it is a big deal to them considering that it is so prevalent in town anyway."

"I wouldn't be so sure about that. Kids talk, and teenagers talk even more. You can bet they're discussing it behind your back and in the hallways. As your assistant principal, I'm warning you that pursuing this type of relationship will harm your career plans. I'd think twice about continuing down the path you're headed," he said.

She started to tell him to mind his own business, but he walked through the doorway and left her there speechless and so angry she swore she saw red. How dare he threaten her career like that. No one other than him seemed the least worried about her personal life. None of the other teachers had said anything.

Jessie looked around at the kids and the other teachers on duty around the room. Were they talking behind her back though? Had one or more of them said something to the principal or assistant principal? Now she was second-guessing her friendships with the other teachers.

She would approach Heather, one of the teachers she thought was close to her, and see if they were talking behind her back. If they were, she would need to do some serious thinking about her future. She loved teaching, but she also loved the guys. If it came down to picking one over the other, what would she do? Jessie wasn't sure.

When the last bell rang dismissing the kids from classes for the day, Jessie gathered her belongings and followed them out of the room. She headed for the teachers' lounge in hopes of catching Heather. The other woman usually had last period free and would sit in the lounge going over lesson plans.

Jessie was in luck, Heather was gathering her things when she walked into the room.

"Hey, Jessie. Glad school's out for the day?" Heather asked.

"Yes. Are you having any trouble with your kids this week?" Jessie asked.

"Not really. Of course most of the kids like science well enough they're at least interested. Why? Are you having trouble? I wouldn't be surprised if you were," Heather said.

Jessie tensed. "Why would you say that?"

"You teach literature. I love the classics, but a lot of kids think they're boring and dry."

Jessie sighed as the tension poured off her like raindrops on a windshield. "Yeah. The boys especially aren't as into reading as the girls are."

"Yeah, when we get to dissecting the pigs, the girls get all weird in my class, so I understand," the other woman said.

"Heather, has anyone said anything to you about me dating Cole and Wesson?" she finally asked.

Heather's brows furrowed, pulling downward slightly. "Not really. I mean there's been some talk, but mostly it's been envious. Why? Has someone said something to you?" she asked.

"Mr. Kelly, the assistant principal, is making noises that it could hurt my career. I was wondering if anyone else felt like what I was doing was wrong."

"That's absurd. You're a great teacher, and nothing you do in your own time should affect your teaching," Heather said.

"Thanks, Heather. I guess I'm sensitive because it's all so new to me. I never would have thought about seeing two men at one time a few months ago. Now I'm in a relationship with two men who make me happy. I don't want anything to sour the happiness. You know?" she asked the other woman.

"Then don't let it. Mr. Kelly is a nosey old man whose wife left him for a younger man years ago. He's pissy about anyone who's happy when he's miserable. Last year he harassed Darryl when he moved in with Matt, his lover. Nothing ever came of that, and it won't with you either. He just made poor Darryl miserable and nearly cost him Matt in the process. Don't let that happen to you." Heather gave her a quick hug. "Got to run. Ned's picking up the baby from his mom's house after work so that gives me just enough time to do a little grocery shopping before they make it home."

Jessie smiled as the other woman raced from the room. Several other teachers walked into the lounge talking about kids and subjects and everything in between. Jessie smiled at them as she passed them in the doorway. No one seemed to be paying her any attention, so she decided that Heather was right. Mr. Kelly was just a nosey busybody who liked to spread his own misery to anyone else he could.

She'd barely gotten in the door of her house when her cell phone dinged alerting her to a message. She pulled up the text and smiled. It was from Cole asking how her day had gone. She texted him back that it had been a good day despite the two unruly teenagers who hated literature.

He sent her an LOL and reminded her they'd pick her up after her fitting for her bridesmaid dress the next day.

She texted back that she couldn't wait. She couldn't. She was just as excited at the prospect of seeing them as she was of spending the time with Brenda and the other women in the bridal party.

Her next text came from Wesson asking her what she was wearing. She laughed and texted back that she was wearing granny panties and a long flannel nightgown. He'd texted back that she sounded like the sexiest granny he'd ever met. That had made her burst out laughing. He was incorrigible.

She read for a while but couldn't get Mr. Kelly's words out of her head. Could he compromise her position or any chances that she could one day land a job with the community college once she'd gotten some good experience in? She prayed he couldn't. What would she do if he could? Jessie wasn't sure. All she did know was that she loved teaching and she loved Cole and Wesson.

Chapter Eighteen

The next week Jessie worked hard with her students to make reading more fun for them. She'd chosen *Lord of the Flies* in hopes it would stir up some excitement with them. So far it seemed to have worked, and she was enjoying her classes again.

Even the two teens who'd disrupted the class the week before seemed to be enjoying this book. Of course it had a little of everything in it from romance to science fiction to fantasy. She hoped their grades would reflect it, as well. Several of the guys in her classes were skating a fine line between pass and fail.

Once school was over for the day, Jessie spent a little time in her room changing the bulletin board out and straightening the books she kept on shelves at the back of the class in hopes some of the kids would find one they enjoyed and wanted to read at home just for fun. It was nearly five when she finally called it a day and gathered her things to head home.

When she walked out into the parking lot, it was to find that her car and Mr. Kelly's truck were the only ones still left in the parking lot. He was leaning into the back seat when she walked up.

"Hey, Mr. Kelly. Is everything okay?" she asked.

He jerked and spun around with a startled expression pulling his mouth into an O shape. Then he looked furious with her, his face drawing down into a scowl.

"What are you staring at?" he demanded.

Jessie frowned and took a step back. "Nothing. I was just asking if you were okay."

She thought she'd caught a glimpse of something shiny in the back seat of his truck, but he was standing in front of it now, so she couldn't see over his shoulder.

"Are you spying on me?" he demanded.

"No. Look, I'm just going to go home now. I can see that you don't need any help."

She started toward her car, but he stopped her by grabbing her wrist. The bite of his fingers into her skin drew a soft cry from her. He immediately let go and scowled at her. His short black hair stood up at the back. Together with his odd behavior, Jessie was a little afraid of him. When she'd first met him back before school had started he'd seemed nice enough, but over the past few months, he'd seemed to change into someone she didn't know.

She backed away from him, afraid to turn her back for some reason. She'd never been particularly afraid of another human being before, but she was of Mr. Kelly now. That thought bothered her. She shouldn't feel that way about one of her bosses.

Just as she started to turn away, he moved to close the back door to his truck, and she caught a clear glimpse of what looked like a rifle lying on the back seat. She nearly hesitated but quickly turned and walked quickly toward her car. What was he doing with a gun in the back of his truck and on school property? They were a gun-free campus. Plus, it had been lying in plain sight on the back seat. Anyone could have seen it or broken in and stolen it.

Jessie locked her car door as she started it up to drive home. More than likely he'd had it covered up before she'd surprised him. Still, why would he have a gun? He didn't strike her as the type to hunt, and it wasn't hunting season as far as she knew.

By the time she'd made it home, she was a nervous wreck and had several text messages from the guys she needed to answer. Jessie gathered her things and hurried into the house, locking the door behind her. She was spooked, and she didn't know why.

Her cell rang just as she'd dropped her things on the island in the kitchen. She answered it in a breathy voice.

"Hello?"

"Hey there, babe. You didn't answer our texts. We were worried," Wesson said.

"Sorry, I was driving. I stayed late at school to tidy up the classroom. How are you guys doing?" she asked.

"Good. Finished painting the barn and damn glad of it, too. Fucking hate painting. Glad the house is mostly brick. Won't have to paint nearly as much when times comes for that."

"Is it hunting season for anything?" Jessie asked before she knew she was going to ask it.

"Hunting season? No. Why?" Wesson asked.

"Nothing. I thought I saw a gun in the back of the assistant principal's truck, but I must have been mistaken. I only caught a glimpse of something long and metal and assumed it was a gun."

"I thought it was illegal or something to have guns on school property," Wesson said.

"It is here. That's why I'm probably wrong about what I saw. Had to be something else." Jessie doubted Mr. Kelly would have broken the rules when it wasn't even hunting season.

"Does he know that you saw something?" Wesson asked in a much quieter voice.

"Well, yeah, but I didn't really see much since he covered it up real quick."

"Was he upset that you might have seen it?"

"He doesn't really like me anyway, Wesson. So yeah, he was upset."

"I don't like it. Why doesn't he like you?"

"Um, well, I think it's because I'm dating you and Cole."

"Has he said anything to you about it?" Wesson asked.

"Yes, he's hinted that I could be ruining my career by seeing the two of you."

"Fuck."

"I don't think he can do anything. Brenda's talked with one of the ladies on the board of supervisors, and she's in a ménage relationship, as well. I honestly don't think he can do anything." Jessie hadn't planned on telling the guys about the man's threats, but now it all seemed more important.

"Is your door locked?" Wesson asked.

"Yes. I always lock it when I'm home. You're scaring me, Wesson. What's wrong?"

"I don't trust this assistant principal. If he is carrying a weapon to school, he's dangerous. I'm going to call the sheriff and get him to look into it. You stay where you are and don't let anyone in but him or us. Got it?" he asked.

"Wesson. I'm not even sure what I saw was a gun. It could have been something else. Do we really need to do this?" she asked.

"What if it was a gun and he's going to go crazy while at work? He could kill or hurt a lot of kids, babe," Wesson said.

"Okay. I just hope this is all a terrible mistake," she said.

When Wesson had hung up, Jessie grabbed a bottle of water from the fridge and walked into the bedroom to change into jeans and a pullover shirt. She needed to rake leaves, but Wesson had made her promise to stay inside with the doors locked. Instead, she curled up in her favorite chair and read on her e-reader.

A knock on her door startled her. She lowered her feet to the floor and walked over to the door.

"Who is it?" She asked.

"It's the sheriff. Wesson called me."

Jessie unlocked the door and let the other man inside. He stood just inside the doorway and closed the door behind him. Jessie waited while he pulled out a pad and pen then told him what she'd seen.

"Like I told Wesson, it might not have been a gun. It was straight and shiny. I don't know why my first impression was that it was a gun, but that's what I thought. It might not have been one at all."

"Why would he have blocked your sight of it if it hadn't been one?" the sheriff asked.

"I don't know. He isn't really a fan of mine. He probably just didn't want me looking over his shoulder. Honestly, I wish now that I hadn't walked over to see if he needed any help."

"Not a fan of yours? What do you mean by that?" the sheriff asked.

Jessie filled him in on the various statements Mr. Kelly had made to her over the last few months. The sheriff wrote everything down on his little pad then nodded and left, reminding her to lock up behind him.

The entire incident, along with the visit by the sheriff, had strained her nerves to the point she needed a long hot bath to relax so that she could sleep that night.

The next day at school proved uneventful. She didn't see Mr. Kelly at all and noted that his truck wasn't in the parking lot when she got ready to leave that afternoon.

Since it was Friday, she and Brenda were planning their usual Friday night pizza night. She changed clothes and was just about to leave when something flew past her shoulder and the sound of breaking glass had her screaming as she ducked down. She instantly knew someone had shot at her. She heard the sound of squealing tires outside the window. She hurried over to look out in time to see a white truck that looked like the one Mr. Kelly had driving off in a spray of gravel. Had her assistant principal really just shot at her?

Jessie hurried over to her purse that she'd dropped on the ground and fished out her cell phone. She called the sheriff's office and reported what had happened. Then she called Brenda to cancel their dinner date. Brenda was nearly hysterical by the time she'd gotten off the phone with her. Then she dialed Cole's phone. He was the calmest of the two men. She didn't want to have Wesson go crazy with worry and end up wrecking on the way to see about her. Because Jessie knew they'd come to see about her.

"Hey, beautiful. How was school?" Cole asked.

"Hey, Cole. Look. I'm fine, but someone shot at my house tonight and—" she began.

"What the fuck? Someone shot at you? Are you sure you're okay?"

"I'm fine. Just scared."

"Did you call the sheriff's office?" he asked.

"Yes. Someone is supposed to be on the way."

Jessie could hear him talking to Wesson in between talking to her. Finally she heard Wesson demand that he put her on speaker phone.

"Jessie, babe. Please tell me you're sitting down somewhere away from any windows," Wesson said.

"I'm sitting in the kitchen waiting on the sheriff. I'm fine, Wesson," she said.

"We're heading your way, darling. Stay on the phone with us until the sheriff gets there," Cole said.

"I'm fine, guys. You don't have to drive all the way out here. I know you're exhausted from working today." Jessie knew it was futile to try and talk them out of coming to see about her, but she tried anyway.

"Of course we're going to come see about you. Someone just shot at you," Wesson said.

She could hear that they were getting in their truck as the doors slammed and one of them started the vehicle. Her heart warmed at the realization that they would always want to take care of her if she'd let them.

"I can hear the sirens now, guys," she said.

"Make sure of who it is before you open that door," Wesson called out over the sound of the truck's engine.

She listened to them until someone pounded on her door. She checked to make sure it was the sheriff's office before letting them in.

"I've got to go, guys. The deputies need me to tell them what happened. I'll see you when you get here," she told them.

"On our way, babe. We're on our way."

* * * *

Wesson was beside himself with anger. Someone had shot at Jessie. Again. Who was this asshole? Why had he focused on her?

The moment they pulled in next to the sheriff's SUV, he was out of the truck striding toward the house. He needed to see Jessie for himself to know that she really was okay. Just thinking about someone harming her had his blood pressure through the roof and his heart racing like a runaway horse.

He could feel his brother right behind him as he reached the door to Jessie's house. A deputy stood just outside on the tiny front porch and put up his hand to stop them.

"Sorry, sir, but you can't go in there," he said.

"Bullshit. That's our woman in there. Someone just took a shot at her, so there's no way you're keeping us out," he said in a low snarl.

"Jessie!" Cole called out.

"It's okay, deputy. You can let them in." The voice of the sheriff came from the other side of the deputy.

Wesson stomped into the room with Cole behind him. The first thing he saw was all the crime scene paraphernalia in the living room. Yellow markers were sitting in various spots around the room, and a large circle was drawn around a hole in the opposite wall from the window. It was just about the spot where Jessie's head would have been had she been walking from the bedroom into the living room. Frigid cold shards of ice cut through his veins.

"Are you okay, babe?" he asked, wrapping his arms around her.

"I'm fine. Just a little shaken up," she said.

He stood back slightly so that Cole could reach her, as well. He turned to the sheriff with a murderous burn in his gut.

"You've got to stop this guy before he kills someone. I take it this time he used real bullets," Wesson said.

"Yeah. He did. He's upped the stakes for sure," the sheriff said.

"What are you doing to stop him?" Cole asked.

"Everything we can, Cole. Everything we can."

"They may have someone to look into now," Jessie said.

"What do you mean?" Wesson asked.

"I saw a white truck drive off right after the gunshot, so now they can look for whoever drives a white truck to question them," she said.

Wesson got the feeling she wasn't saying everything. She wouldn't look him in the face when she spoke. Did she know more than she was telling them? What about the sheriff? Had she told him whatever she was hiding? He'd wait until later to question her. He didn't want to upset her more than she already was, though he had to be honest, she was handling it all pretty damn well.

"There can't be that many white trucks around here to check," Wesson said.

"We're going to investigate everything, Wesson. There's no need for you to worry about it. Let us do our jobs," the sheriff told him.

"This is the second time someone's shot at Jessie. Now they're using deadly force and not just darts," he snarled.

"Easy, Wesson," Cole said. "Let them handle this. We'll watch after Jessie from now on."

"As soon as the sheriff is finished with you, pack a bag, Jessie," Wesson said. "You're coming home with us."

Chapter Nineteen

Jessie relaxed between the two men as they escorted her out to their truck. Both Wesson and Cole walked with her so close beside them that she nearly stumbled. They weren't taking any chances that whoever had shot into her house wasn't still out there waiting for her to emerge from the house to try again.

Cole helped her up into the truck and waited by the door until Wesson had climbed into the driver's seat before he got into the back passenger side of the truck. The sheriff had promised to let them know when they had a suspect in custody. She'd told him about what she'd seen at school concerning the assistant principal and how he'd been harassing her about dating Wesson and Cole. She hadn't told the two men in her life though.

The drive to their place was made in near silence. The rich darkness was so thick it felt as if she could cut it with a knife, yet there were thousands of sparkling stars in the sky above. Jessie loved that about living outside of the larger towns. Bright city lights blinded people to the beauty of nature.

"You're awful quiet, darling. Are you sure you're okay?" Cole asked her from the back seat.

"I'm fine. Just can't believe someone tried to shoot me. It just doesn't seem real somehow," she said.

"You were so damn lucky, babe. My stomach flips just thinking about what could have happened," Wesson said.

He pulled the big truck behind their house to the back door. Cole jumped out and looked around before opening her door and helping her down. Wesson grabbed her overnight bag from the back seat and followed them into the house.

"Want something to drink?" Cole asked.

"I could really use a Diet Coke. I didn't get my usual fix after work," she joked.

"Cole, why don't you take her into the living room while I get us all something to drink?"

Jessie followed with her hand clasped tightly in Cole's as he led her into the other room. She sat on the couch with Cole on one side of her. He leaned over and kissed her on the cheek then the forehead.

"We could have lost you, hon. I don't think I could have stood losing you. We just found you," he said in a soft voice.

"But I'm fine. Nothing happened to me. I'm going to have to get someone over to repair my window and my wall though."

"We'll take care of that for you. You don't have to worry about a thing," Cole said.

"Take care of what?" Wesson asked as he brought in two beers and Jessie's beloved Diet Coke.

"I was telling her we'd handle getting the repairs done on her house for her," Cole said.

"Absolutely. You don't need to worry about anything," Wesson said. "Now. Why don't you tell us what you wouldn't tell us back at your house?"

"What do you mean?" Jessie asked, knowing full well what he was talking about.

"I saw the little eye exchange you had with the sheriff when you were telling us about the white truck. What are you hiding?" Wesson asked.

"The sheriff is going to take care of it," she said.

"Take care of what?" Cole asked, setting his beer on the coffee table.

"The white truck looked a little like the one the assistant principal drives. It doesn't mean it was him, just that he drives a white truck," she said.

"And this is significant why?" Wesson asked.

Jessie sighed. He could tell she was still holding out on them. She was terrible at lying even by omission.

She finally relented and told them about her run-ins with the man she'd had prior to that. Both men were outraged and chastised her for not confiding in them about the trouble she'd been having with the man.

"That's harassment, babe. You should have gone to the principal and complained about his actions," Wesson told her.

"I wasn't sure how the principal would feel about us dating either. I thought that if I left it alone he'd eventually get tired of bothering me. After I found out that there was someone on the board that was also in a ménage relationship I didn't worry so much anymore," she said.

"You shouldn't have had to put up with that kind of environment at work," Cole said.

"If it turns out that the assistant principal is the one who's been shooting at cattle and people, then I won't have to worry about it again," she said.

"You should have gone straight to the sheriff with what you thought you saw. Even if it had turned out not to be a gun, it was the best thing to have done. Maybe you wouldn't have nearly been killed if you had," Wesson chided.

"I know you're right, but I was afraid I was letting my feelings for the man interfere with what I was seeing. I didn't want to bring more attention to myself by getting the sheriff involved." Jessie sipped her drink.

"Are you hungry?" Cole asked.

"Not really. I could use a nap I think. I'm exhausted. I guess all the excitement wore me out," she confessed.

"Come on, hon. We'll lie down with you until you fall asleep. You're probably crashing after the adrenaline rush," Cole said as he stood.

Wesson pulled her to her feet, and she let them lead her to the bedroom. She stood still while they pulled back the covers on the bed and undressed her so that she crawled into bed nude. The two men removed their boots and shirts and climbed on top of the covers to hold her until she finally drifted off.

* * * *

Jessie breathed in the scent of something cooking and opened her eyes. The room was dark except for a sliver of light coming from the bathroom door where they'd left it cracked. She stretched and groaned at how good it felt being in their bed. The only thing nicer would have been to have both of them there with her.

She climbed out of bed and searched through her overnight bag for a long T-shirt and underwear. The tantalizing smells coming from the kitchen had her stomach clenching in hunger. It had been a long time since lunch earlier that day. She had no idea what time it was now, but she was hungry.

The sound of voices carried to her as she walked out of the bedroom and down the hall.

"I'm just glad they finally caught the bastard," Cole said.

"When I think that he was at that school near Jessie every day, I get a sick feeling. He could have hurt her at any time," Cole said.

"Who? What's going on?" Jessie asked, walking into the room.

Cole turned from what he was doing at the stove and smiled at her. "Hey there, honey. Did you sleep well?"

"I did, but what's going on?" she asked.

"They arrested that assistant principal, Mr. Kelly. He had a tranquilizer gun and a rifle in his truck. The fool hadn't even tried to hide them other than throwing a blanket over them in the back seat," Wesson said.

"So it was his truck I saw leaving tonight," she said.

"Yes," Cole said.

"I'm so glad this is all over with now. I've felt as if there was a target on my back ever since he shot me with that dart," Jessie confessed.

"Did he say why?" she asked.

"He hasn't said much of anything according to the sheriff, but they've been digging and evidently his wife left him for two men and moved to New Mexico with them. He'd claimed it was one man, a younger man, but hadn't admitted to anyone that it was two men. He's been harboring a deep-seated anger against threesomes ever since," Cole told her.

"We're so lucky he didn't seriously hurt anyone," Jessie said.

"I'm just thankful he didn't hurt you. You came so close last night. If you'd been standing in the wrong place it could have been much, much worse," Wesson said.

"But I wasn't, and everything is fine now," she said.

"Hungry?" Cole asked. "I've got bacon, eggs, and toast ready."

"Starved," she admitted.

They ate while talking about what they wanted to do the next day. Jessie reminded them that she had a bridesmaid dress fitting that afternoon so she'd have to go back home to get her car to meet the others at the bridal shop.

"We'll take you and pick you up. We'll eat dinner in town after your fitting," Cole suggested.

"If you're sure you don't mind." Jessie loved that they were so attentive.

In fact, she loved a lot about them. They were kind, easy going, and fun to be with. While Cole was less serious and more teasing, Wesson was steady and solid in his mannerisms. She liked that she could depend on him to be there when she needed him. Both men sincerely seemed to love her, and she definitely loved them. She loved them so much it scared her. The thought of losing one or both of them twisted her insides with pain and fear. How had she gotten so attached to them in such a short period of time?

"Why the serious face, love?" Cole asked.

"Just thinking that I love you both so much it scares me."

"Why?" Wesson asked. "Why does it scare you?"

"I don't know what I would do if I lost one or both of you. We haven't really known each other more than a few months, and already I feel as if I'd die if I lost you," she admitted.

"We feel the same way, babe. You mean the world to us. We don't want to ever think about living without you in our lives," Wesson said.

Cole stood and carried their plates to the sink. He reached down and took Jessie's hands in his.

"This isn't really the place or the time, but I can't stand it. I have to ask," Cole began.

"Ask what?" Jessie asked.

Wesson jumped to his feet and walked over to where Cole had Jessie standing next to him. He took one of her hands from his brother and carried it to his lips for a soft kiss.

"Jessie, would you marry us?" Cole asked, looking down at her with so much love in his eyes that Jessie felt tears burn in hers.

"You want to marry me? Really?"

"Absolutely," Wesson said. "We want you with us for the rest of our lives."

"I love you guys so much. Yes. I'll be your wife." Jessie squealed when both men crushed her between them.

"Back off some, Wesson. We'll suffocate her if we aren't careful. She's such a tiny thing." Cole squeezed the hand he still held.

"I'm not tiny at all," she said with a teary laugh.

"You're the perfect size for us, babe," Wesson said.

"How does this work? I can't marry both of you at one time. It's not legal," she pointed out.

"You'll marry Cole because he's the oldest, and then we'll have a ceremony for the three of us with our friends," Wesson told her.

"Oh God," Jessie said with a soft cry.

"What?" Cole and Wesson asked at the same time.

"Brenda's going to go crazy planning the wedding, and she isn't even married yet." Jessie smiled through the tears of happiness that filled her eyes. "I can't wait to tell her."

"So pick a date," Wesson said.

"Now? Pick a date right now?" she asked.

"Yeah. I want it officially written down before we do anything else. I want to program it on my phone and write it on the calendar in the kitchen," Wesson said.

"I don't know. How about a July wedding? Nothing fancy, just a small ceremony. That would give us time before school starts again," she suggested.

"June," Cole said.

"What? That's barely after school lets out," she squealed.

"Okay, okay. July. When in July?" Cole asked.

Wesson pulled up the calendar on his phone, and they settled on the weekend after the fourth. It would give them nearly three weeks after school was out to plan and another three weeks before school started. Jessie couldn't believe she was planning her wedding already. Brenda was going to go crazy when she told her about it the next day.

"Come to bed, babe. I need to hold you," Wesson said, tugging on her hand.

"I want to be held by you. You and Cole," she admitted.

The second they were in the bedroom, Wesson pulled her shirt over her head then wrapped her in his arms. Neither man was wearing a shirt, but they both still had on their jeans. She reached between them and started unfastening Wesson's jeans.

"I need you naked. Both of you," she said, tugging at his pants.

Cole was already out of his, pressing against her back with his nude body. She moaned at how good it felt to have the man flush against her back, skin to skin. The heat of his warmed her cooler skin. She leaned back as Wesson pulled down his jeans and stepped out of them, leaving them lying on the floor where they dropped.

"Get her in bed, Cole," Wesson said.

"Already working on it," Cole said as he walked her toward the bed with him behind her.

Jessie hit the edge of the mattress and climbed up on the bed. She turned around to watch her men climb on the bed behind her. She loved how their eyes were heavy with desire. Desire for her, for what they could do together. The sight of them nude with their hard bodies and muscular builds sent shivers down her spine.

"Lie back, babe. I want to taste you. Lie on the bed for me so I can lick that pretty pussy," Wesson said.

Jessie drew in a deep breath and did as he asked. The thought of him going down on her had her pussy weeping with need. He spread her legs wide to accommodate his wide shoulders and lifted her ass with his hands as he ran his tongue up her slit. Jessie gasped at the sensation of his tongue against her wet folds.

"Damn you taste good, babe. I love the way you taste," Wesson said.

Cole wasn't about to be left out. He'd climbed on the bed next to her and relaxed on his side so that he could reach her breasts with his hand and his mouth. Jessie wrapped one arm around his shoulder and pulled him to her.

"Kiss me, Cole."

He smiled and claimed her mouth with his, moving his lips over hers then licking them so that she opened to him. As soon as she did, he plunged his tongue deep inside her mouth and slid along hers. She loved how he kissed, as if touching every part of her was important. He sucked on her tongue then on her lips before pulling back and turning his attention to her breasts.

Jessie threaded her fingers through his hair as he sucked in a nipple and drew on it. The sensation had her toes curling and her back arching even as Wesson licked over her clit with his tongue.

"Oh God," she whispered in a hoarse voice.

"I could eat this wet pussy all night, babe. You taste like spicy honey." Wesson drew his tongue down her slit once more then speared her pussy with two fingers.

Jessie clamped down on his fingers, loving that she had something to hold on to as he drove her higher with his tongue. Already that heavy pressure that built just before an orgasm was filling her body with need.

Wesson thrust his fingers in and out of her before turning them and rubbing back and forth until he found that sweet spot deep inside her cunt that made her wild beneath him. Once he found it, he massaged it relentlessly. Every stroke sent her higher and higher until the combined feel of those fingers, his mouth on her clit, and Cole's mouth and fingers on her nipples drove her over the top as her orgasm exploded around her.

Jessie screamed until no sound came out of her mouth with the sheer pleasure they brought her. Her body bucked, and she dug her fingers into their scalps as she jerked between them. The orgasm ripped guttural sounds from her throat until she was hoarse and coughing.

"Easy, babe." Wesson climbed up on the other side of her, petting her as she spasmed between them.

"God, I love to watch you come undone like that," Cole said in a soft voice. "You're fucking amazing."

"Too good," she finally managed to get out. "Always feels too good."

"It's never too good," Wesson said. "I can't wait to get inside that tight pussy. You're going to come for us again. Aren't you, babe."

"Oh God. I'll die if I come like that again," she said.

Wesson climbed over her and lifted one leg over his arm. "You're soaking wet, babe. Love how wet you get when you climax."

Jessie groaned when he slowly began inching his way inside of her. He was so thick and hard. It felt wonderful to have him filling her. She lifted her hips to meet him as he finally made it all the way inside of her. She felt full and antsy with the need to move. His hard length pulled back then shoved back in, startling a yelp from her.

"Okay, babe?" he asked.

"Yes. You feel so good inside of me," she said. "So good."

"I want that pretty mouth around my dick," Cole told her.

He cupped her cheek with one hand and guided his cock to her mouth with the other one. "Are you going to suck my dick for me, hon?" he asked.

"Yes. Let me taste you, Cole."

She opened her mouth and took his long shaft into her mouth. He was salty and hard against her tongue. He pushed in then pulled out as she sucked on the bulbous head before sliding her tongue over the slit at the tip of his cockhead. His swift hiss of pleasure made her smile around his length.

Together, the two men fucked her in slow even thrusts. She took Cole's cock as deep into her throat as possible then swallowed around him so that he called out her name. Every time Wesson's dick hit her cervix, she squeezed down on him so that he growled in pleasure. The three of them moved like dancers on a stage as each of them gave pleasure and received it in return.

Cole's thrusts in and out of her mouth became frenzied as he grew closer to his climax. Jessie reached up and took his balls in her hand and gently rolled them as she sucked hard on his shaft. He threaded his fingers into her hair and pulled on it as he called out.

"Fuck. I'm going to come, hon. Swallow it all, Jessie. Swallow my cum."

Jessie felt the first salty taste of him hit the back of her throat. She took him down as far as she could and drank his seed as he filled her mouth and throat with long ribbons of it. When he'd finished, he pulled out and collapsed next to her against the headboard but continued to massage her scalp with his fingers.

"That was so fucking hot, darling. I almost feel like I could pass out I came so hard," Cole said.

"Hold on, babe. I'm close, too. I want you to come first though." Wesson lifted both of her legs over his arms and began pounding into her.

"Wesson. I'm close, I'm so close," she cried out.

Jessie didn't think it was possible she could come any harder than she already had, but when Wesson rubbed his thumb across her clit while thrusting his thick dick in and out of her, she wasn't sure anymore. The climax building deep inside of her felt massive and all-consuming. It frightened her a little.

Wesson set a punishing pace as he pinched her clit between his thumb and finger, and Jessie's world exploded behind her eyes. She hadn't even realized she'd closed them until bright blinding lights illuminated her eyelids as she screamed out in pleasure. The orgasm ripped through her like a runaway train tearing through the station. Her hearing went first then her vision as she lost consciousness for a few seconds.

Jessie didn't think she'd ever regain the ability to breathe normally again, but finally it all settled down so that she could think and talk again.

"That was amazing," she finally got out.

"Better than amazing," Wesson said.

"Better than anything," Cole added.

"I love you, guys. I love you both so much," Jessie told them.

"And we love you," Wesson told her.

"I still can't believe that you're all mine," Jessie confessed.

"Why not?" Cole asked.

"Because finding one man worth loving is hard, but finding two seems impossible. But I found the two of you, and I'm the luckiest woman in the world," she said.

"And we're the luckiest men in the world to have you," Cole said.

Jessie snuggled between the two men and vowed to tell them how she felt every day for the rest of their lives together.

THE END

WWW.MARLAMONROE.COM

Siren Publishing, Inc.
www.SirenPublishing.com

Lightning Source UK Ltd.
Milton Keynes UK
UKHW010011271118
333016UK00007B/995/P

9 781642 435436